First Published in Great Britain 2017
By Mills & Boon, an imprint of HarperCollins*Publishers*
1 London Bridge Street, London, SE1 9GF

© 2017 Jennifer F. Stroka

ISBN: 978-0-263-06912-9

Printed and bound in Great Britain
by CPI Antony Rowe, Chippenham, Wiltshire

MARRIED FOR HIS SECRET HEIR

BY
JENNIFER FAYE

Award-winning author **Jennifer Faye** pens fun, heart-warming, contemporary romances with rugged cowboys, sexy billionaires and enchanting royalty. Internationally published, with books translated into nine languages, she is a two-time winner of the RT Book Reviews Reviewers' Choice Award. She has also won the CataRomance Reviewers' Choice Award, been named a TOP PICK author, and been nominated for numerous other awards.

Visit the Author Profile page
at millsandboon.co.uk for more titles.

For Caitlin

From one book lover…
to another :-)

PROLOGUE

Paris, France

IT SHOULD HAVE been the most amazing night of her life.

Elena Ricci swept her long blond tresses over her shoulder as she stepped backstage at the Paris fashion show that had just concluded. She should be on cloud nine, but instead worries brought her feet back down to earth. With a borrowed diamond necklace and matching earrings now returned to the jeweler and her crystal-embellished gown returned to the designer, she was ready to call it a night.

"Are you heading straight to the party?" a female voice called out behind her.

Elena turned to find a young woman smiling at her. Try as she might, Elena couldn't put a name to the face. "No. I'm going to pass on it."

"But you have to go," the beautiful young woman with flowing black hair said. "As the face of the line, you're like the guest of honor. Tonight is your night."

"I'm sure you'll all have fun without me. I'm just not up for a party."

"Ah, I bet you have other plans." The young woman flashed her an I-know-what-you're-up-to smile. "I'm sure he'll be worth it."

He? There was no he. The last guy she'd had the misfortune of dating had been a liar and a cheat. Elena had sworn off men after that debacle. Who needed the hassle?

"There is no guy," Elena clarified.

"Really? Then who's the man waiting for you at your station?"

Elena didn't bother answering. She just started walking. If it was Steven, she was having security escort him out.

She'd told him in no uncertain terms to get out of her life. And she'd meant it.

When she neared her station, the man had his back to her. "I told you I didn't want to see you again."

The man turned. "Is that the way you greet all your friends?"

Heat rushed to Elena's face. Before her stood the Earl of Halencia, Luca DiSalvo, her childhood friend. "I'm sorry. I, uh, thought you were someone else."

"I think I feel bad for the other guy."

"Don't. He doesn't deserve anyone's sympathy." She rushed forward and gave Luca a hug, finding comfort in his strong arms. And there was something else—a warm sensation that set her stomach aflutter. But she refused to examine the reason for her elated reaction.

The truth of the matter was, she'd grown used to shoving aside her emotions when it came to Luca. Their friendship meant the world to her, and she wouldn't do anything to risk it—even if it meant they would never be more than friends.

He pulled back and smiled. "That's better."

She looked deep into his tired eyes. There was something bothering him. This wasn't just a casual visit. Luca didn't do those. For him to come here unannounced, it meant something had happened—something big.

"What is it?" she asked. "Is it your father?"

Luca shook his head. "It's my mother."

"Your mother?"

Luca drew in a deep breath. "They caught her murderer. Actually, my sister did. Can you believe it? After all these years, it's finally over."

Elena wasn't sure how to react. On one hand, she was relieved they'd solved the crime, but she also knew how tough the years following the heinous crime had been on Luca and his estranged family. She couldn't imagine how he must be feeling at this point.

After the murder, Luca had withdrawn from everyone around him—including her. When he'd finished high school, he'd moved away. Soon after, she'd done the same and moved to Paris. Their friendship dwindled to an occasional phone call or an annual visit over coffee at a small café when Luca was in Paris on business.

Over the years, she'd told herself not to take the distance personally. It was Luca's way of dealing with the unimaginable grief. But she couldn't deny that losing the close connection with her best friend had hurt—a lot.

A million questions bubbled up within her. And yet she remained quiet as he gave her the highlights of how Annabelle had caught the murderer. The story was truly stunning.

"Annabelle just phoned me." His gaze didn't quite reach Elena's. "And I just needed to tell you." He paused as though considering his words. "I guess if I'd been thinking straight, I should have realized your mother would tell you."

Elena reached out and briefly squeezed his hand. "I'm glad you're the one who told me."

"You are?"

She nodded. "I'm so sorry this happened to you and your family. I hope the murderer's capture will help in some small way."

"Me, too."

There was something different about him. Instead of the usual cool aloofness that he wore like armor, he was uneasy, and there was a glimmer of vulnerability in his blue-gray eyes. Had he come here for yet another reason?

Refusing to let herself imagine that Luca was ready to become a part of her life again, she busied herself. She bent over and slipped on a pair of bright white tennis shoes with pink laces. Now that her makeup had been wiped away and the glittery, gauzy creations had been returned to the clothes rack, she felt like herself. Plain old Elena.

When she straightened, she found Luca staring at her. Her heart thump-thumped. She swallowed hard. "What is it?"

"Nothing. I was just looking at you."

Worried that she'd missed removing some of the sparkly blue eye makeup they used to make her up as a fairy for the new magical fashion line, Elena turned to the mirror. She didn't see anything but her own complexion. Her cheeks were a little rosy from the cleanser, but it was all her in the reflection. So why had Luca been looking at her so strangely? She shrugged it off.

"Can I persuade you to stay long enough to eat?" She hadn't eaten a bite all day. She'd been a nervous wreck about the show, and now that it was over, she was ravenous. "Or we could get one of your favorite pizzas from Pierre's and take it back to my flat."

"Your flat?" Luca shook his head. "Not going to happen. I hear you have some exciting news." He moved to the end of her makeup table and retrieved a champagne bottle. "We have to celebrate. It's nonnegotiable."

She wasn't sure either of them was up for celebrating. Before she could vocalize her protest, Luca popped the cork and Elena watched as pink bubbles rushed down the side of the bottle. Luca reached for a champagne flute and filled it up.

"For you." He held the glass out to her.

She accepted it. Luca was certainly acting out of character. Her gaze lowered to the glass as the pink bubbles rose and popped. If Luca and the designer of the line Elena now represented only knew of the mess she'd made of her private life, they wouldn't help her celebrate being chosen as the new face of the Lauren Renard line.

Elena felt like a fraud. They all thought she was so good—so deserving. But she was none of those things. Her judgment was way off where men were concerned. She'd been too trusting—too open—and in the end, she'd been lied to in the worst way. Now she didn't trust herself or men.

"Elena?"

She glanced up. Her gaze met Luca's. Tears suddenly rushed to her eyes. She blinked repeatedly, refusing to unleash the turbulent emotions that had been threatening all day.

"Hey, none of that." Luca raised his glass. "This is a moment for celebrating."

Elena forced a smile to her lips and lifted her glass.

Luca held his glass close to hers. "To the most amazing, wonderful tomboy I've ever known. And I might add that you clean up pretty good, too."

Her mouth gaped as their glasses clinked together. "That's not fair. I haven't been a tomboy since we were kids."

His eyes studied her. "I have one question for you."

"You can ask it, but I reserve the right not to answer." A nervous shiver rolled through her stomach. Had he heard about her romantic debacle? She groaned inwardly before taking another drink of champagne—a much bigger drink.

"When did you become so beautiful?" Luca's gaze caressed her, leaving her insides aflutter.

Heat rushed to her cheeks. "Be careful, Luca. If I didn't know better, I might think you were flirting with me."

"I am."

Her heart lodged in her throat. What had come over him? Luca was a constant flirt, but always with every other woman in the room. And now she didn't know how to react to him.

Luca grabbed the champagne and refilled their glasses. "Drink up. I'm taking you out on the town tonight. I'm going to show off the hottest lady in Paris."

He thought she was hot?

Maybe he was referring to the blush that had engulfed

her face. She resisted the urge to fan herself. Instead, she gulped another mouthful of bubbly.

Luca was far too sexy, and he was saying all the right things to sneak right past her meticulously laid defenses. If she wasn't careful, this evening was going to blow up in her face.

She swallowed hard. "But I'm tired—"

"Trust me. What I have in mind will wake you right up." He winked at her.

Her heart skipped a beat. She didn't know what to say. Instead she busied herself with another sip of champagne. As the alcohol hit her empty stomach, she realized that it wasn't her wisest idea and set aside the glass. "It's not that big of a deal."

"Of course it's a big deal. It's a huge deal." He smiled at her like he had something in mind. He'd been giving her that look since they were kids playing in the fields of wildflowers on the palace grounds in Mirraccino, and she knew it meant he had mischief on his mind. "We have to celebrate. And I have the perfect idea."

Why did it suddenly feel like Luca's reaction to her new role for the world-renowned Lauren Renard line was over the top? After all, Luca was an earl. He was royalty, for goodness' sake. His father was the Duke of Halencia. And Luca's mother had been the sister of the King of Mirraccino. Elena knew that her accomplishments didn't come close to stacking up to Luca's impressive lineage.

"Luca, it's really not that big of a deal." Heat rushed to her cheeks.

"Quit being so modest. You worked hard for this." He walked over to her and put his arm over her shoulders. "I'm proud of you. Just wait until my sister hears about this. In fact, she was just asking about you."

"She was?" When he nodded, Elena said, "Tell her I said hi."

"I will. Right after I tell her about you being world famous and the face of her favorite clothing line."

In truth, being the face of such a renowned line was truly a turning point in Elena's career. She wouldn't just have her face on the middle pages of a magazine. She would now dominate the covers. Her calendar would be filled with photo sessions. Finally, she was no longer just the daughter of the King of Mirraccino's secretary or the tomboy who followed Luca all around the palace grounds and played football with him until long after the sun set. She was now a successful international model—for however long it lasted.

"But after your news, I'd really understand if you didn't want to make a big deal of it."

"Indulge me," Luca said.

"What's that supposed to mean?"

"It means while you were taking your final stroll down the catwalk, I was on the phone."

"And? You were finding out the location of the next hot party?" She had no doubt there were parties with so many notable people in town this week for the line reveal, but that just wasn't her scene.

"There's only one party on my mind." He looked at her rather intently.

Her heart raced. "Luca, when did you become so mysterious?"

"Mysterious?" There was a glint of mischievousness reflected in his eyes. "I've been accused of a lot of things, but never that."

"Well, then out with it. What plans did you make?"

"Trust me. You'll find out soon enough."

She moved to retrieve her purse and turned back to say something when his lips landed on hers. That wasn't supposed to happen. Her heart jumped into her throat. So why wasn't Luca pulling away? Why wasn't she?

Maybe if she had held still just a moment longer, his

kiss would have landed on her cheek. Yeah, that was probably it. But now that they were in this awkward situation, neither moved. Could he hear the pounding of her heart?

Over the years, she'd wondered what it'd be like to feel Luca's mouth pressed to hers. But she'd never, ever thought that it would actually happen.

And then his lips moved over hers, tentatively and slowly, as though figuring out where they went from here. Her pulse raced, and any rational thoughts slipped out of reach. At last, her dream was coming true.

Her purse slipped from her hand as she reached out to him. Her fingers slid beneath his gray sports jacket to the black T-shirt beneath. As her palms slid over the defined contours of his chest, a moan swelled in the back of her throat.

Oh, yeah... This kiss—this moment—was so much better than she'd ever imagined. She definitely approved of this change in Luca.

His arms wrapped around her, pulling her close. Need, wonderment and eagerness consumed her. The rush of emotions was more intoxicating than the bubbly they'd just shared.

As their kiss intensified, his tongue slipped past her compliant lips. She leaned in closer, pressing the length of her body against his. If this was a dream, she didn't want to wake up.

A whistle followed by applause from the stage crew had her reluctantly pulling away. She wasn't sure what she expected to find when she gazed into Luca's face. Perhaps disappointment or regret, but instead he was smiling at her. It was one of those smiles that made his eyes twinkle.

"Are you ready to go?" Luca whispered into her ear, sending goose bumps racing down over her body.

"Um...yes."

"Good. I want to make this a very special evening for you."

It was already special. That kiss had been so unexpected and so much better than she'd ever imagined. This was a different side of Luca, and she liked it—she liked him—a lot.

After retrieving her purse from the floor, she slipped her hand into his and they rushed out the door. She refused to second-guess this decision. It was her one chance to be something so much more than Luca's friend.

At last, he'd seen her as a desirable woman.

CHAPTER ONE

Nine weeks later, Mirraccino Island, the Mediterranean

SHE'D HEARD IT said that you can never go home again. Maybe she should have heeded that warning.

Elena stared at herself in the full-length mirror in her bedroom at her parents' modest home on the royal estate of Mirraccino. This trip had not been her idea. It had come about rather suddenly when her mother broke her leg.

Her mother had called to say that she couldn't get around on her own, and since Elena's father was needed at the palace, her mother was home alone all day. As their only child, it was up to Elena to return home. And though the timing wasn't ideal with the start of the new campaign for the Renard line, Elena had worked feverishly to reschedule all of her appointments. She was more than willing to help her mother, who'd always been there for her.

But unbeknownst to Elena, her mother had exaggerated her condition. The fact that her mother had played on Elena's emotions was unusual, so she let it pass without comment. The truth was she didn't make it home often enough.

Don't think about it. Not this evening.

She hadn't even unpacked yet when her mother had handed over an invitation printed on heavy cream stationery sealed with a deep purple royal crest. A little confused, Elena had opened it, surprised to find that she'd been invited to Lady Annabelle's engagement festivities. The invitation had said the event was to be intimate and to dress casually.

Now, two days later, she'd tried on every single dress she'd brought with her from Paris at least twice. Some were too revealing. Others were too flashy. And some were too formal. What exactly did one wear to dinner at the palace?

She'd never been in this situation before. Although she was the daughter of the king's private secretary, she wasn't the type who received invitations to royal events. And this wasn't just any party. It was a weeklong series of events. And her mother had taken it upon herself to post an acceptance on Elena's behalf.

Knock. Knock.

"Come in."

Her mother smiled as she entered the room. Her long dark hair was pulled back and tucked up at the nape of her neck. Only powder accentuated her natural beauty. "I just wanted to see if you needed any help getting ready."

"I'm the one who should be asking if you need anything."

Her mother waved off the concern. "I'm fine."

"Isn't Father home yet? I thought he might stay with you while I'm out for the evening."

The smile slipped from her mother's face. "I don't see your father much lately."

Elena had noticed her father's increased absence. "What has him so busy?"

"The same thing as always—the king."

"Oh." Elena knew from growing up that her father kept his work to himself. And that was probably why he was the king's most trusted employee. "I'm sorry. I had hoped the king would be back to normal by now."

"I had hoped the same thing. Nothing has been right since they arrested that murderer. The news hit the king really hard."

"I'm sure it was quite a shock to learn there was a murderer wandering through the palace all those years."

Her mother shuddered. "I don't like to think of it. Your father saw that criminal every day. Just the thought—"

"Don't go there. It's all over." Elena hoped to reassure her. "Father is safe."

Her mother sent her a weak smile and nodded.

Elena turned back to the full-length mirror. She'd finally settled on a little black dress. It wasn't anything special. But the black suited her mood. She'd been sullen and reserved ever since her night with Luca. It had been just one more mistake on her part—a total error in judgment.

The only right decision she'd made was agreeing to be the face of one of the world's hottest designers. The work was now coming in droves. In fact, there were so many requests for appearances and photo shoots that she couldn't do them all. But once word got out about her condition, it would all end.

She was pregnant with Luca's baby.

Pregnant. The word still sounded so foreign to her.

She'd always kept track of her cycle—a little tick mark on her day planner. With the hectic schedule of a new campaign, she hadn't noticed right away that her timely cycle had suddenly drifted off course. But referencing her day planner to schedule future shoots, she'd stumbled across the missing tick mark. Her heart had clenched before panic ensued.

Four home pregnancy tests later, her worst fears had been confirmed. She was pregnant with Luca's baby. At this point, only Elena and her doctor knew the truth. And for the moment, that was how it'd remain.

"Is that what you're wearing to dinner?" her mother asked, studying Elena's black dress. A decided frown came over her face. "Don't you have something more cheerful?"

For some reason, her mother's disapproval decided Elena's attire for her. "I like this."

"You're awfully skinny." Her mother clucked her tongue disapprovingly. "While you're home, you need to eat more.

Thin is nice, dear. But when a man wants to wrap his hands around you and—"

"Mother, stop." She couldn't believe her prim and proper mother was talking about a man having his hands on her. It just sounded so wrong to hear her mother talk about sex. *Ew!*

"Really, Elena. I didn't think you were a prude, especially with those sexy outfits you model."

"I'm not a prude. It doesn't mean I want to talk about—about that—with you."

Her mother smiled. "I didn't think people your age were so shy talking about sex."

"Enough. You're really making me uncomfortable here."

"Okay. Okay. I'll stop."

"Thank you."

Ding. Dong.

Elena looked at her mother. "Are you expecting anyone?"

"Not that I recall."

"I'll get it." Elena made a move toward the door, immensely grateful for the interruption.

Her mother held up a hand. "You stay and finish getting ready. I'll entertain your date."

"I thought you didn't know who was at the door?"

"I, ah, just remembered." Her mother's gaze avoided hers.

"Really? That's interesting, because I don't recall making a date."

"I know, dear. That's why I arranged for one. After all, you don't want to show up at the palace all alone."

Stunned by her mother's matchmaking, Elena stood slack jawed as her mother used her crutches to maneuver out of Elena's bedroom. She even pulled the door shut behind her.

Elena didn't know what shocked her more—her mother's agility or the fact Elena had a date that evening and her mother hadn't even told her the man's name. At least with her mother doing the matchmaking, Elena knew the man would be honest and a gentleman.

The only problem was Elena didn't want a date. She was perfectly happy going to the palace alone. This wasn't the good old days when it was unseemly for a twenty-five-year-old woman to be seen in public without an escort.

She had to put a stop to her mother's meddling. After all, she'd returned to Mirraccino to take care of her mother, not the other way around.

Elena glanced back at the mirror. She turned, giving a side view. Would anyone be able to tell she was pregnant? She didn't think so. She wasn't far along. And so far she'd been able to avoid the dreaded morning sickness. A little nausea now and then and being a bit more emotional than normal were her only symptoms.

She turned away from the mirror and slipped on a pair of platform stiletto heels adorned with crystals. The added height to her five-foot-ten stature always gave her a boost of confidence. The peekaboo toes would give a glimpse of her pedicure. Thankfully, she'd had a nail appointment just before she left Paris. She'd hoped it would lift her spirits. It hadn't.

She pulled open the bedroom door and headed downstairs. "Mother, I—"

The words died in her throat. There, making chitchat with her mother, was Luca. Her heart lurched into her throat. How could this be? Luca never visited Mirraccino. And yet here he was, smiling and laughing with her mother.

He looked incredibly handsome with his dark hair cropped short on the sides and back while the top was a bit longer. He wore a charcoal suit that amplified his already broad shoulders—shoulders where not so long ago she'd rested her head. She squelched the thought as fast as it came to her.

Sans a tie, the top two buttons of his white dress shirt were unbuttoned, revealing a glimpse of his tanned chest and the gold chain that held his St. Christopher medal. He'd been wearing that necklace—a gift from his mother—almost as long as Elena had known him. She knew it meant a great deal to him.

He looked like he was ready to step onto a runway in Paris or Milan. He was certainly photogenic enough. He had it all—the looks, a title and money. He wanted for nothing. Even though he'd settled down with a job in the financial sector, she knew he traveled routinely. With his home base in Milan, he often traveled throughout Europe to the States and then to Australia before he started the expedition once again. And he certainly never lacked for companionship.

She should have known that Luca would be her mother's idea of an appropriate date. Her mother would like nothing better than to have her marry into the royal family. But Elena had made it clear that would never happen. She'd had enough of men. They only wanted one thing. Once they got it, it was game over and they were on to their next conquest.

Not so long ago, Luca had been the love 'em and leave 'em type. And the aftermath of their night together hadn't convinced her that this particular leopard had changed his spots. It was best that she trod carefully where he was concerned.

"Hello, Elena." Luca placed a practiced smile on his face, but there was a flicker of something dark in his eyes. In a blink it was gone, leaving her to wonder if she'd imagined it.

"Hi. I…I didn't know you were back on the island."

"I was told by my sister that if I didn't make an appearance for her engagement celebration, she would track me down and it wouldn't be pretty when she found me."

"I can imagine your sister following through on that threat."

"Me, too. So here I am."

"And since your appearance was last minute," her mother interjected, "Luca kindly agreed to be your escort. Isn't that right, Luca?"

His Adam's apple bobbed. "Yes, that's right. It looks like we're both without dates this evening."

"But that doesn't mean my mother should have imposed on you." Elena sent her mother a pointed look.

"I didn't." Her mother feigned innocence.

Elena's gaze narrowed on her mother, not believing her. "And I suppose Luca is now psychic and knew I'd be here this evening without a date?"

Elena could feel Luca's gaze on her, but she refused to face him. She was already embarrassed enough. How could her mother do this to her?

"I was just trying to help," her mother said. "Luca came round the other day to check on me. He'd heard about my accident, and he wanted to make sure I was okay."

It sounded innocent enough, but how that translated into a date was another story. "And that's when you hatched this scheme to impose on his kindness."

"Young lady—" her mother's voice took on a sharp edge of indignation "—I don't now, nor have I ever, hatched a scheme. I merely mentioned that you were flying in to town."

"And I suggested that we go to the dinner this evening— together." Luca was no longer smiling.

He was mad at her? She was only trying to undo her mother's meddling. She was certain her mother had more to do with this arrangement than she was letting on. Wait. Had he just said he was the one who'd wanted to go to the dinner with her?

Elena's gaze shifted to Luca. But it was like he had built a wall between them, and she wasn't able to read his thoughts. Drat! She felt as though she was standing on shifting sand and she just couldn't get her footing. The best thing to do was let him off the hook, gently.

"I appreciate your thoughtfulness, but you don't have to bother," she said, watching his eyes grow darker. "I don't mind going to the palace by myself."

"What about the palace?" Her father stepped through the doorway in his standard black suit, collared white shirt and black tie.

"Luca came to escort Elena to the dinner at the palace." Her mother beamed. "Isn't that wonderful?"

Her father's face was pale and drawn. Dark circles had formed under his eyes from being on call for the king at any hour of the day or night. Elena wished her father would set some boundaries in his life, but he insisted that his duty was to the king, and he could not be deterred.

Everyone stood quietly waiting for her father to speak. It wasn't like him to be so quiet. Usually he would tell her to have a good evening and be on his way.

"Are you all right?" Elena asked her father.

"I'm fine. Just a little tired." Her father moved to stand in front of Elena. He leaned forward and pressed a feathery kiss to her cheek. "But I'm feeling better now. How could I not with my wonderful family around me?"

Elena's mother nodded toward Luca. "Aren't you going to say anything to our guest?"

Her father grunted as though he'd forgotten. He turned to Luca. "Don't do anything to hurt my girl. Or else..."

Her father didn't finish the threat, but Luca's rigid stance and the firm line of his lips said that he'd gotten the message.

"I'll go clean up for dinner," her father said and moved toward the stairs.

"Shall we go?" Luca asked.

Elena had to try one last time to call off this awkward

date. "As I was saying before, I really don't mind arriving alone."

Luca sighed. "Ah, but see, I do mind. I hate showing up at these family events alone. There will be questions about who I'm dating, if it's serious and if I ever plan to settle down and get married. I'd rather avoid all that."

So she would be doing him a favor? By what? Being his decoy? A shield?

No. No. No.

She wasn't comfortable with any of those titles. Elena had enough of her own secrets. She didn't need to be drawn into anyone else's drama.

The past few months in Paris had consisted of making one bad decision after the other. It had gotten to the point where she had no faith in her own judgment. And now that she was pregnant, she had to make the right decisions. There was an innocent baby counting on her. She had mixed emotions about her unexpected condition. How could she tell Luca she was pregnant when she didn't even know how she felt about it?

That was why her mother's request for her to return home couldn't have come at a better time. She had hoped some downtime would clear her head. At the time, she'd had absolutely no idea that Annabelle was having a big celebration or that she would include Elena in the festivities.

Her gaze landed on Luca. He looked uncomfortable and anxious to be anywhere but here. Things had definitely changed between them. Where there had once been an easiness, there was now this crackling tension. If she needed any confirmation that they could never go back to how they used to be, this was it.

Tonight, she would be nervous enough being a guest at the palace. She really didn't need the added awkwardness she felt around Luca. If only he wasn't so insistent on being a gentleman and escorting her.

"I'm not quite ready to go." When he didn't say anything, she added, "I don't want to make you late."

"I don't mind waiting," he said. "It'll give me some more time to talk with your mother."

Her mother smiled. "And I just made a fresh batch of those amaretto cookies that you enjoy."

"They're my favorite," Luca said. "And I haven't had them in a very long time. You really are the best in the kitchen."

Her mother shook a finger at him. "You have grown up to be quite a flatterer. I'll just go get you a few."

"If you don't mind, I'll join you."

Her mother nodded and set off for the kitchen with Luca following closely behind. Elena stood alone in the entryway. What exactly had just happened?

CHAPTER TWO

LUCA COULDN'T TAKE his gaze off her.

Had Elena always been this beautiful?

Thankfully she'd turned her head to stare out the car's window at the passing fields of wildflowers while in the background the setting sun painted the sky with streaks of orange, pink and purple. But tonight Luca was in no mood to appreciate nature's beauty.

In the weeks since he'd last seen her in Paris, he'd convinced himself that everything about their evening together had been blown out of proportion by the champagne. He just couldn't accept that he was attracted to his childhood friend. He couldn't allow that to happen, because they could have no future.

He wasn't into commitments.

Not now. Not ever.

But there was something about Elena that pulled at him...even to this day.

And then he remembered how he'd woken up the morning after they'd made love and heard Elena sniffling. The sound had ripped him apart. No one had ever cried after spending the night with him. And the fact that it was Elena, of all people, made the situation so much worse.

He hadn't moved for an indeterminable number of minutes. Her muffled sobs had sliced through him. Clearly she'd thought their night together had been a mistake. Unable to think of anything to say to comfort her, he'd continued to breathe deeply as though he'd still been asleep. Each breath had been painful, as his entire body was tense. The memory was still so crystal clear.

He had done that. He had made Elena cry. And he felt awful.

If only he hadn't let things get out of hand. But he'd thought she'd been having a good time. Still, he should have resisted kissing her. He should have made their friendship the priority. If he'd been thinking clearly, he would have realized there would be no coming back from holding her all night long.

He swallowed hard as the limo glided through the estate to the palace. The ride only took a couple of minutes, but with Elena so close to him, time seemed to stand still. For the first time, he wasn't sure what to say or what to do.

Boy, he'd really messed things up between them. He resisted the urge to rake his fingers through his hair. He needed to look his best for the professional photos his sister would undoubtedly insist upon.

On second thought, this date is not a good idea. Not good at all.

"Are you sure about this?" Elena asked.

"Yes." *Liar.*

She arched a brow. "You don't sound certain."

This was where he should reach out and squeeze her hand to reassure her, but instead he didn't move. He didn't trust himself to touch her. The images of their night together were still in the forefront of his mind.

He'd really mucked things up. The truth was he didn't want to be Elena's escort, but when her mother had mentioned Elena's return to the island, he'd been caught off guard. And when her mother had mentioned the party, Luca had spoken without thinking.

And now, well, all he wanted to do was sweep Elena into his arms and pick up right where they'd left off back in Paris. He wanted to feel her eager lips beneath his— ready and willing.

He halted his thoughts. This wasn't like him. When he ended a relationship, he moved on without looking back.

With Elena there had been no moving on. Since that night, no other woman had interested him.

When he closed his eyes, it was Elena's face he saw. It was the memory of her lips that tormented him. How was he ever supposed to get her out of his system?

So he didn't dare look at Elena right now. He refused to act on those desires. She'd made it abundantly clear that she regretted their night together—no matter how hot and steamy it had been.

He just needed to focus on something else—anything else. His mind drew a blank. Perhaps he should start a conversation. Yes, that was a good idea. But what should he talk about?

"I was surprised to hear you were back on the island." There—that sounded normal enough.

She shrugged. "I didn't have much choice, considering I thought my mother truly needed me."

"I take it she exaggerated her injuries?"

Elena nodded. "By the sound of her on the phone, she was on death's door."

Luca smiled. "I can imagine."

"What does that mean?" Elena suddenly sounded protective of her mother.

"I just meant that your mother would do anything to get you home."

"And how would you know? You're here even less than I am."

He shrugged, not certain he wanted to admit that he talked with her mother often enough. At first, Elena's mother had concocted any excuse possible to call him, but as time went by, he got used to hearing from her. He actually looked forward to it, because she would fill him in on all of Elena's accomplishments.

"I just remember how she used to be—always wanting you to stay close to home."

Elena shrugged. "She finally accepted that my future wasn't in Mirraccino."

"Speaking of which, how did you get time off from your new campaign to fly here?"

Elena glanced away. "I…ah, had a break in my schedule."

There was something more she wasn't telling him, but he didn't push. If she wanted him to know, she'd tell him when she was ready. The fact she was even speaking to him, he took as a positive sign. Maybe there was hope for their friendship after all.

The car pulled to a stop in front of the palace. Though he'd been staying here since he arrived a couple of days ago, he didn't want to attend this dinner any more than Elena. But he refused to disappoint his sister. He'd already hurt her enough by leaving home and allowing extended gaps between visits. He knew Annabelle wanted her family reunited, and now that their mother's killer had been caught, she thought it would fix everything.

It wouldn't.

Luca had witnessed too much. Experienced too much. And he couldn't be the son that his father needed—and perhaps deserved.

But now that Annabelle was getting married, hopefully she'd stop longing for the family she'd lost. When a family member was murdered, it seemed for the most part that families reacted in one of two ways. The horrific event either drew them together—the family against the world. Or it splintered them apart—each finding their solace in a different way. His family had been the latter.

Luca's car door swung open, interrupting his thoughts. It was for the best. He didn't want to dwell on how he'd disappointed his sister repeatedly over the years. Tonight was to be a celebration. And he would put on his biggest and brightest smile, which shouldn't be too hard since their father, the duke, was not to be in attendance. Tonight was an informal gathering of friends and some family. Annabelle wanted her groom to meet the people who had meant a lot to her while she was growing up.

An enormous wooden door with brass fixtures swung open. An older gentleman in a black-and-white tux stepped outside to greet them.

Elena put her hand on Luca's arm, pausing him from getting out of the car. She leaned over and whispered, "That's so strange."

"What is?" Luca glanced around, but he didn't notice anything amiss.

"That the butler is there to greet me—well, us. That's never happened in my whole life."

Luca smiled and shook his head. "I'm glad it makes you happy."

"It does."

Luca alighted from the car and turned back. He held out his hand to help Elena to her feet. "So what do you think?"

"I think that no matter where I go, this palace is the most beautiful building." Her gaze focused on the palace and not him. "What do you think? You've traveled even more than me. Have you ever seen anything so amazing?"

Luca turned to study the expansive building. He had honestly never really looked at the place. He was embarrassed to admit that he'd taken the centuries-old palace for granted. Over the years, it'd been expanded upon, which included the addition of the towering turrets. Though once used to keep an eye out for approaching enemy ships, they were now more a decoration and painted with stripes of yellow, pink, aqua and gold.

"It really is remarkable," Luca said, his gaze straying to Elena. "A beauty unlike any other that I've ever found."

Just then Elena glanced at him, and he turned away. Did she know he was no longer talking about the palace?

He hoped not. He didn't want to give her the wrong idea. They'd had their chance together—as brief as it might have been. There was no way of recapturing it. He refused to even consider it. Okay, maybe he had considered it, but he wouldn't act upon his desires.

Even if their lovemaking hadn't made her cry, they didn't belong together. He couldn't make her the promises she deserved. And he wouldn't have any woman waiting around for him when he had absolutely no intention of making a commitment.

Therefore, it was best that he shove aside those tempting images of her in his arms with that wanton desire reflected in her eyes. He swallowed hard. Could they ever be friends like before? He was feeling less assured about that with each passing moment.

The butler stood aside. "Welcome, Miss Ricci. It's good to have you back."

"Hello, Alfred. It's good to be back."

Luca held out his arm to Elena. She paused and looked at it as if she wasn't sure what to do. Boy, he really had messed things up between them.

"Go ahead," he encouraged. "I promise not to bite."

A small smile lifted the corners of her very desirable lips. She tentatively slipped her hand into the crook of his arm. When an unfamiliar sensation pulsed up his arm and settled in his chest, he stilled his body. He refused to give any indication that her touch affected him. Because it hadn't. Not really. It was just nerves. He was just worried about doing something to drive his best friend even further from him.

"Are you ready?"

Elena nodded.

Her face was void of emotion. He knew that look. It was her working face—the look she wore when she was strutting down the catwalk in some amazing outfit. He couldn't rightly describe any of the fashions she wore, because when he googled her, he was always caught up by the beauty of her face. It didn't matter what hair color or stylish cut she was sporting—ever since their night together, he'd been captivated by her.

He took sure strides up the steps to the open palace door. Inside, there was a host of palace staff to greet them and escort them to the dining room. It was odd, considering Luca had been running through this palace with his host of cousins since he was in diapers. That seemed so long ago now.

A flash went off, momentarily blinding Luca.

Elena came to a standstill. She released his arm. "The press is here?"

"Not that I know of."

Elena took a step back. "I should have expected this. Coming here was a mistake."

Luca glanced around. The photographer moved out of the dining room. "It's not the press. It's a private photographer. My sister is sentimental and wants to have pictures to remember these events."

Elena's worried gaze met his. "You're sure?"

He nodded. "Since when did you become so shy? I thought the camera was your friend."

"You thought wrong." And with that Elena brushed past him and headed into the dining room.

What had just happened? His radar was going off. Something was definitely amiss. And it frustrated the heck out of him that he'd wrecked their relationship to the point where she wouldn't even open up to him.

He rushed to catch up to her. "Tell me what's bothering you."

"Nothing."

"If it's nothing, why won't you even face me?"

She didn't stop. "It's nothing," she called over her shoulder. "Just drop it."

"Tell me what it is and I'll fix it if I can."

She stopped and turned to him. Wearing an indifferent expression like a mask, she said, "I don't know why you think I need help."

Luca reached out and grasped her arm before she could wander off. "I know things aren't right between us, but I also know you really well, and no matter what you say, I know there's something wrong—something big."

Elena yanked her arm from him. "You should concentrate on your sister. This is her big night."

As though his sister had heard her name mentioned, she rushed over to them. Annabelle's face was aglow with happiness. "Elena, I was so excited when I heard you were back on the island." She reached out and they quickly hugged. "Thank you so much for coming."

A strange sensation coiled through Luca as he watched the easy smile light up Elena's face. Elena certainly hadn't done that when she'd spotted him at her mother's house. In fact, her reaction had been quite the opposite.

He didn't know why he let it bother him. There were plenty of other women out there who would be happy to have his company. If only he had the slightest bit of interest in those other women.

He inwardly groaned with frustration. He turned away and went in search of something to drink. He wasn't really thirsty, but it was certainly better than watching Elena make nice with everyone—everyone but him.

He had to quit letting her get to him. He needed to withdraw. Wasn't that what he'd promised himself after his mother's murder? To keep people at a safe distance?

That was why he'd packed up and moved away from Halencia and Mirraccino. It hurt too much when people he cared about were torn from his life—whether by murder, grief or something else. He just couldn't go through that again.

And though he'd missed his sister and Elena while he'd been traveling, he'd been able to distract himself. He was always on the go. A new adventure. A new challenge. That was exactly what he should do now—set off on a new expedition. But he couldn't. Not yet.

Until the week was over, he had to make the best of this situation. And then he would be gone. He would return to Milan. He would make plans for some daring feat and forget all about these unwanted emotions.

CHAPTER THREE

AT LAST SHE was an invited guest.

Elena had never thought the day would come when she would be invited to the palace. It was the final confirmation that she'd gone from being a nobody to a somebody. She was no longer the shy child who was left out of all the elaborate royal birthday parties and the other celebrations Luca and his sister attended.

After waiting a lifetime for this moment, she was surprised to find it wasn't nearly as satisfying as she'd imagined. Truthfully, she wasn't enjoying herself. She was in no frame of mind to take part in such a celebration. Her life was a mess, and she had a feeling the worst was yet to come.

At dinner, Luca had been seated at the other end of the extremely long table. There was no chance of him probing her with his eyes—searching for answers to his unspoken questions. The problem with hanging out with her former best friend was that he could still read her like a book. And she just wasn't ready to open up to him.

During the dinner, she'd witnessed Annabelle's bubbly happiness. It was then that Elena made her decision. She would delay telling Luca about the baby until the end of the week. By then, the celebration would be over and the fallout from her announcement couldn't ruin this happy occasion.

The delay would be best for everyone. Until then, she'd have a chance to figure out her life plan and to find the right words to soften the blow for Luca. Not that she wanted anything from him—that she'd decided. But he was the father of her baby, and he deserved to know the truth.

She glanced around, finding Luca engaged in a conversation with Prince Demetrius. This was her chance to quietly slip away from the party. After all, who would notice?

Besides possibly Luca. But they'd been doing their best to avoid each other all evening. So perhaps he'd be relieved to realize that she'd gone.

Luckily, having spent her youth avoiding the guards and servants, she knew her way around the palace. She slipped into the hallway. A quick check both ways let her know that the coast was clear. Her gaze latched on the French doors at the end of the hallway. Although freedom was within reach, she forced herself to walk at a reasonable pace.

She inhaled a deep breath, hoping to calm her rising nerves. All she wanted now was to escape the curious looks and the inevitable questions regarding her showing up as Luca's date. When her hand grasped the brass handle, she glanced over her shoulder. So far, so good.

She let herself out onto the patio that was surrounded by the royal gardens. She looked left and then right. All alone. She breathed her first easy breath all evening. Whatever had made her think that coming here would be a good idea?

She moved to the far end of the patio and leaned her palms against the cold concrete balustrade supported by dozens of tiny pillars. The entire palace was a work of art. And just now the gardens were aglow beneath the full moon. It was breathtaking—

"There you are." Luca's voice came from behind her.

The breath caught in Elena's throat. She'd been so close to making a successful escape. Why had she stopped? Maybe because she knew this would be the last time she would be welcome at the palace. Once word got out about all her ill-advised activities, no one would want her around—most especially Luca.

Steeling herself, she leveled her shoulders, plastered a smile on her face and turned. "Luca, I didn't hear you approach."

"And I didn't hear you say anything about sneaking off into the night." His dark brows were drawn together.

"Who said I was sneaking away?"

"I did. And you were."

The smile was getting harder and harder to maintain. "Really, Luca? Sometimes you imagine too much."

"Don't try to brush me off. I know you, Elena. You put on a pretty good show this evening for the other guests, but I can see you aren't happy."

"Of course I'm happy. I'm honored that your sister still thinks so highly of our childhood friendship to invite me to such an event."

"Annabelle likes everyone." And then, as though he realized how that might sound, he added, "But you meant a lot to her, especially when our mother died."

Elena had tried her best to be there for both Luca and Annabelle, but he'd pushed her away. It was as if overnight Luca had built a wall around himself and no matter how hard she tried, there'd been no scaling that wall. Eventually she gave up.

"I don't belong here," Elena said.

"What? Of course you do."

She wasn't going to argue with him. Her gaze strayed to the sweeping steps that led to the garden. "I made an appearance, and now it's time that I go. Please tell your sister I had a good time."

Luca crossed his arms over his broad chest. "Tell her yourself."

The abruptness of his comment caught her off guard. "I…I will." A written message would be so much easier than a phone conversation where inevitable questions would arise. "I'll drop her a note tomorrow."

"This isn't about you fitting in. It's about us. Isn't it?"

She met his unwavering gaze. "Why would you think that?"

"Because I really screwed up in Paris. It was all a big mistake. I wasn't myself that night. And if you give me a chance to make it up to you, I swear it'll never happen again."

The more he tried to explain, the more his pointed words poked at her hope that they'd get past this awkward stage. But now she knew the unvarnished truth. And it was worse than she'd thought.

Having no response for him, she turned to continue walking.

"You can't just walk away," he called out.

Why did he have to keep pushing? He wasn't going to like anything she had to say. It was best to keep moving. She took another step.

"Elena, what is it going to take for you to forgive and forget?"

She turned, catching the frustration written so clearly on his face. "You don't understand. The past can't be that easily erased."

"What are you saying?" He stepped closer to her. "Elena, what is going on?"

Elena pressed her lips together. She'd said far more than she'd intended at this juncture. And now she'd aroused Luca's suspicion. There was one thing that Luca excelled at and that was ferreting out the truth. If she didn't get out of here soon, her secret would be out. And this royal scandal—the earl having a baby with a commoner, the daughter of the help— would be the talk of the palace and beyond.

She knew it would happen sooner or later, but she'd been hoping for later, after Annabelle's moment in the spotlight. After all Annabelle had been through tracking down her mother's murderer and then being held at gunpoint, her friend deserved this bit of happiness.

"I'm not leaving here until you talk to me," Luca said. "So out with it."

"I just meant we can't pretend that night didn't happen."

He didn't say anything for a moment, as though he were

considering the sincerity of her statement. "I understand. But I don't want to lose our friendship."

Before she could say a word, the sound of voices and approaching footsteps interrupted. Elena glanced past Luca and spotted Prince Alexandro alongside another of Luca's cousins. The prince glanced up and surprise flashed in his eyes.

"I'm sorry. We didn't know anyone was out here," Prince Alexandro said. "We'll go."

"No. Stay. You aren't interrupting anything," Elena hastily responded.

The prince's gaze moved between her and Luca. "You're sure?"

Luca hesitated and then nodded.

"Good," the prince said, approaching them. "Luca, we need you to settle a disagreement."

The men quickly got into a heated discussion about the upcoming European football season. Elena immediately tuned out the conversation. She wasn't a sports fan unless it was auto racing. There was just something about a hot guy and a fast car. Her mind immediately conjured up Luca in a sleek racecar. The image definitely worked for her. But just as quickly as the image came to her, she dismissed it.

With the men now deep in conversation, Luca had his back to her. She took advantage of the moment to follow through with her original plan to steal away into the night. Trying to act as casual as possible, she quietly strolled down the steps and entered the garden.

When she reached the other side of the garden, she slipped through the gate and entered the open field illuminated only by moonlight. At last, she was free.

With her hand splayed over her midsection, she said, "Don't worry, little one. We'll tell your father. The time just has to be right."

* * *

A late-night phone call was never a good thing.

In Luca's case, it always meant that his life was about to take a turn for the worse. He doubted tonight would be any different.

"Father?"

"Luca, you answered." Surprise rang out in his father's voice.

Was he that bad at accepting calls from his father? Perhaps. He had started to avoid his father's calls because the man kept hounding him to step up and take his place in the family business—a position Luca didn't feel comfortable assuming.

"Are you all right?" Luca asked, rubbing the sleep from his eyes.

"I'm coming to Mirraccino first thing in the morning. We need to talk."

"Is that code for you want to discuss how I'm wasting my life? If so, you're wasting your time—"

"I'm serious, Luca. It's imperative that we talk." There was a weariness to his father's voice that he'd never heard before. And it concerned Luca more than he'd expected.

"Can't you just tell me now?"

"No. We need to do this in person. And don't tell your sister. She'll find out soon enough, but for now she deserves to enjoy her engagement."

"Understood."

"Good. I'll see you first thing in the morning. Don't sleep in."

"I won't."

When they disconnected, sleep was the very last thing on Luca's mind. His father was far from melodramatic. In fact, after his mother's murder, his father had been the only calm person—perhaps too calm. At the time, Luca had resented the fact that his father hadn't fallen to pieces. In that moment, he'd been certain his father didn't love his mother. Not like he should have loved her.

That was the moment when Luca pulled back from everyone. Convinced that love was just an illusion, he'd refused to become a victim of romance and happily-ever-after. Because when the haze of lust lifted, someone would walk away and someone would get hurt.

And as much as Luca believed his father had not loved his mother, as the years slipped by, his doubts set in. His father never moved on with his life. He never remarried. Luca wasn't even sure his father dated. If he did, he used the utmost discretion. And the few times that Luca had returned to their home in Halencia, it remained the same. His mother's belongings were still where she had left them. It was so easy to pretend that she was just out for the day. It made Luca wonder if he'd misjudged his father. Had his father loved his mother in his own way?

Sleep was elusive for the rest of the night as Luca stared into the darkness. He knew as sure as the sun would rise that his life was about to change dramatically. It left him restless.

And then there was the matter of Elena.

She'd gotten away from him tonight. He didn't know what was bothering her, but he intended to find out. It wasn't like Elena to act so mysteriously.

Tomorrow there was a picnic. He wasn't sure what else Annabelle had planned for the day, but he was certain it wouldn't be boring. Nothing about the day would be mundane, because he had every intention of once again escorting Elena to the event. It would give them a chance to finish their prior discussion.

There was something going on with Elena, and he felt driven to find out what had this international fashion model cowering from the cameras. Perhaps it wasn't any of his business, but the worried look reflected in Elena's eyes haunted him.

He might not have been around much in the past few years, but he was here now. By helping her, he might be able to assuage some of his guilt over losing control in Paris. If he did, perhaps they could part on good terms.

CHAPTER FOUR

THE NEXT MORNING Luca paced back and forth in the palace library.

It was time he let his father in on his life choices. Luca couldn't help but wonder what his father would think of the fact that he'd gone back to school and received his degree in business management. He knew he was destined to run the family's citrus business one day. And he wanted to be prepared. In fact, for the past several years, he'd been working his way up in an investment firm in Milan.

Perhaps he should have told his father all of this sooner. He'd intended to, but it never worked out. Every time they got together, they argued. His mother used to say that they butted heads so much because they were so much alike. Luca had always taken it as an insult. He had never wanted to believe that he was as stubborn and infuriating as his father—

"Luca." His father's voice came from behind him.

Being so deep into his thoughts, Luca hadn't heard his father approach. He turned toward the doorway. "Hello, Father."

"At last we talk. You really ought to get a new phone so your messages don't get lost."

Luca had noticed the messages, but he kept putting them off for one reason or another. "I've been busy."

His father's dark, bushy brows drew together. "Humph... How can you be busy?"

Luca inwardly groaned. Did his father always have to think so little of him? And then he realized that it was partially his fault. His stubborn pride had kept him from revealing to his father that he'd followed the path his father had wanted him to take in the first place.

Luca cleared his throat. "What did you need to talk about?"

"Is that how you greet your father?"

"It's not like we're the mushy type. That's Annabelle's area."

His father broke out in a hearty laugh, surprising Luca. He had absolutely no idea what he'd said that was so amusing.

His father quickly recovered his composure. "Apparently you've spent as little time around your sister as you have me. Let me enlighten you so that you are not shocked this week. Your sister has grown up into a strong woman and a bit of a spitfire."

That would explain the adventure she'd gone on to track down their mother's murderer. "I'll definitely keep that in mind." Still not comfortable in his father's presence, he said, "Now, what did you want to talk about?"

His father's formidable presence melted away as his face seemed to age almost instantly and his broad shoulders drooped a bit. The duke closed the library door and headed for the tray of coffee and biscuits that had been left by the staff.

His father busied himself pouring a cup of coffee. "Would you like some?"

"I'm good." Then as an afterthought, Luca added, "Thanks."

He wasn't used to his father being thoughtful. This meeting must be serious. And right now, he was too wired. Adding caffeine to the mix would be a mistake.

After his father fixed his coffee with some sugar and a bit of cream, he turned. He took a long swallow before returning his cup to the saucer. "You need to move home."

Luca's body tensed. That was it? No explanation. Nothing but an order. Throwing around his authority was so typical of his father. But he must have forgotten that Luca was no longer a child to be bossed around.

"No." If his father would talk to him differently, he'd explain to him that he already had a job with responsibilities.

His father's eyes flared with anger. "You don't understand. You don't have a choice. It's time you stop partying and live up to your responsibilities."

"And if I don't?"

"You'll be cut off from your funds."

This was where he had his father. "If you hadn't noticed, I haven't touched that bank account in years."

His father's mouth gaped. A second passed before he regained his composure. "I...I didn't know. How are you getting by?"

Luca knew that he could continue to keep his father in the dark, but what good would that do? After all, he wanted to prove to his father—and himself—that he had changed. This was a good starting point. "I'm an account manager at an investment firm."

"You are?" His father leaned back against the table as though for support. The news appeared to have knocked him off balance.

Luca couldn't deny that he found a bit of satisfaction in being able to surprise his father. "Yes. I went back to school, earned my degree and I've been based in Milan ever since. But my work takes me around the globe."

"I see."

No *I'm proud of you.* Or *I'm happy for you.* His father seemed to absorb the news as though he'd just been told there was rain in the forecast.

"Well, I'd like to say that it's been great catching up, but we never were good at casual conversation. So if that's all, I should be going." Luca turned to the door.

"Wait. You can't go. Not yet." His father's voice took

on an ominous tone, causing Luca to turn back. "You need to know…"

When his father's voice faded away and his gaze centered on the coffee in his cup, Luca became suspicious that there really was a problem. His father never acted coy. Whatever it was had his father acting out of character.

"I need to know what?" Luca asked.

His father's hand shook just a bit as he turned to place the coffee cup on the table. When he turned his attention back to Luca, his eyes were dark and unreadable. "The family business is failing."

Failing? The grove of lemon trees had been in his family for five generations. It was a tradition. It was their history.

Luca had to be certain he understood his father. "And this is why you want me to move home?"

His father sighed. "I'm not getting any younger. It's time I pass the torch to you and step down. But before I do this, I need to know that you're up to the challenge. Are you ready to settle down and do the work necessary to save our business and our home?"

Sure, he'd been gone for a long time, but in all honesty, he never meant to be gone forever. His home in Halencia was where he planned to settle…eventually. He'd just never thought anything would happen to it. He always imagined it'd be there waiting for him when he was ready to accept his destiny.

But now his father was looking to him for help. What did his father think Luca could do that he hadn't already done himself? Luca didn't have any answers, but he did know this was his chance to prove to his family that he was someone they could count on.

After all, they had world-renowned lemons with a delicate taste and low acidity. Surely there had to be a market for them. They'd never had a problem in the past.

It would be so easy to turn his father down and go back

to his comfortable life in Milan. After all, he hadn't created the problem. It wasn't his responsibility to fix it.

But this was the first time his father had ever turned to him for help. How could Luca walk away from that? He was certain his mother would plead with him to let go of his pride and help his father.

It wouldn't be easy moving back to Halencia. His father might talk of retirement, but Luca knew his father wouldn't do it. The business was all his father had left. It was in his blood. So how would Luca work side by side with such a stubborn man?

Before he made up his mind, they needed to get a few things straight.

"Why do you want my help?" Luca asked, needing his father to admit that he needed him.

"I...I just told you."

"No, you told me the company is in trouble, but you didn't say why you turned to me."

His father hesitated. "Fine. I need your help. I can't do it alone. Is that what you want to hear?"

Luca nodded. "Yes, it is. And there's one more thing."

"I'm afraid to ask."

"Then just listen. If I succeed, you'll sign over the position of president to me."

His father's dark brows gathered and his mouth opened, no doubt to protest.

"You did say that you were planning to step down, didn't you?" Luca knew as sure as the sun was going to rise tomorrow that unless an agreement was in place, his father would never step down. Once the company was back in the black, his father would no longer have a reason to hand over the reins.

His father sighed as he shrugged his shoulders. "Okay. You'll be president if you succeed."

"And you'll put this all in writing?"

The duke's shoulders grew rigid as his bushy brows drew together. "My word isn't enough for you?"

"Let's just say, this way there will be no room for mis-understandings."

His father studied him for a moment. "The Luca who left here years ago never would have asked for such a contract."

"I was young then. And my mother had just died. It's not fair to throw that in my face—"

"Slow down. You didn't let me finish. I was going to add that I am impressed. You've grown up to be a man who isn't afraid to stand his ground, even against his father. I just hope you have that much resilience and guts when it comes to turning around the business."

"I will. Trust me."

Luca hoped he sounded more assured than he felt at that moment. His entire future and his family's legacy hinged on him pulling together a new business plan. And it was just starting to sink in that this endeavor might be much more important than proving himself to his father.

He had just signed on to save their home—the place where his ancestors had lived for generations. The place that was filled with memories of his mother. The thought tugged at his heart.

And at the moment, he didn't have a plan. He had to come up with one fast. And it had to be good—no, it had to be great.

At last her mother was resting.

Elena breathed a sigh of relief. Her mother was far too active. It was difficult to get her to stop and elevate her ankle like the doctor had told her to do. And her mother looked wiped out. She'd said her ankle throbbed at night and it kept her awake.

Today, Elena had promised to sit with her to watch an old black-and-white movie starring Cary Grant. Her mother seemed pleased with the suggestion, seeing as her father wasn't one for movies. He'd rather play checkers or cards to pass the time.

It was only a matter of minutes into the movie when her mother drifted off to sleep while sitting upright on the couch. Elena put a throw blanket over her and was on her way to the kitchen for another cup of coffee when there was a knock at the door. Not wanting her mother to wake up, she rushed to the door and opened it.

There, standing before her, was Luca in a blue button-up shirt with the sleeves rolled up, white shorts and boat shoes. He looked as if he'd just stepped off the deck of a luxury yacht. Dark sunglasses hid his eyes from her.

She ran a hand over her hair, realizing that she hadn't bothered to do much with her appearance that morning. "Luca, what are you doing here?"

"I thought we could walk together to the picnic."

"But last night—"

"You left before we finished our conversation. So are you ready to go?"

"I'm not going."

"You can't back out. It's a weeklong celebration and everyone on the invite list is expected. I was told this personally. Apparently my sister thinks I might skip out on her. So if I have to go, you do, too. And that includes the dinner and dance on Saturday."

"Your sister must be so excited." What did one even wear to such an affair? She wasn't certain, but she guessed frilly hats might be involved. She didn't own any.

"I'll give my sister credit for bringing together all our childhood friends. It was a good idea. And don't worry, the dance isn't a full-on ball. I imagine she's saving that for the wedding. Anyway, are you ready to go?"

He had to be joking. She glanced down at the ratty T-shirt she'd found in her old dresser as well as a pair of cutoff jean shorts. "Um, no. I'm looking after my mother. She had a rough night."

"I'm sorry to hear that. We could always stay here? I'm sure Annabelle would understand."

"But I wouldn't." Her mother's voice was immediately followed by the tapping of her crutches.

Elena turned to her mother. "But I'm here to take care of you."

"I can take care of myself. And if you go, perhaps I can take a nap without being interrupted."

"Sorry. I didn't mean to disturb you." Luca at least had the decency to look embarrassed.

Her mother waved away his worry. "I'm glad you stopped by. I remember a time not so long ago when you and my daughter were inseparable."

Was her mother trying to set them up again? Heat rushed to Elena's face. Of all the times for her mother to try to play matchmaker, this was the worst.

"That was a long time ago, Mother." Elena hoped to dismiss that subject.

"Not that long ago by my standards. You two got into all sorts of mischief. I was never sure which one of you was the instigator. I think you took turns, but regardless, you were always a mess by the time you got home. I can't begin to tell you how many outfits you ruined with mud. I was certain that one day you two would end up together—"

"Mother..." Elena lowered her voice, willing her mother to stop.

Elena didn't know if it was the embarrassment or something else, but suddenly her head felt a bit woozy and her stomach lurched. She pressed a hand to her forehead, hoping to settle her head. This wasn't good. Not good at all.

At least it wasn't the cramping she'd experienced just after she'd learned she was pregnant. That scare had sent her running to her ob-gyn. The doctor assured her that everything was normal, but she'd agreed to do a sonogram so Elena could see it with her own eyes.

The sight of her own itty-bitty baby with a heartbeat had brought tears to her eyes. She'd had them print out a photo that she carried in her purse everywhere she went. She was surprised she hadn't worn out the photo from holding it so much.

"Elena, are you feeling all right?" Her mother sent her a worried look.

Elena willed her body to cooperate. If only it would listen. "Sure. I'm fine."

Her mother studied her. "I don't know. You're a bit flushed and you haven't been eating much. Maybe you should stay home today and rest. I could call my friend and tell her that we'll play cards another time—"

"Nonsense. I'm fine. Nothing to worry about."

Her mother sent her a look that said she didn't believe her. With her mother, it was hard to say if the news that Elena was pregnant with the earl's baby would be welcome. It would either make her mother extremely happy or horrify her that it hadn't happened in the proper manner.

"There you go again," her mother said. "You look like you're about to pass out."

Why did her mother have to pick now, of all times, to make a fuss over her? Elena swallowed hard. "It's just a little warm in here."

"Warm?" Her mother's frown increased.

Elena chanced a glance at Luca, who was unusually quiet. He was staring right at her as though also trying to determine what was up with her. She just hoped that after their time apart his keenness at reading her thoughts would be skewed. After all, surely he wouldn't be able to figure out her condition just by looking at her.

Perhaps an outing was best. She was anxious to avoid

her mother's questions. "I really need to change my clothes. I don't want to be late."

Once upstairs and with the bedroom door closed, Elena took her first easy breath. It wouldn't be long now until her mother figured out that she was pregnant. And then what? Did she fess up that it was Luca's baby? Her mother would insist on a wedding. And that wasn't going to happen. Neither Elena nor Luca was interested in marriage. As it was, Luca had been doing enough backpedaling after their night together to make it clear that he didn't want more than friendship with her.

So where did that leave her? Saying she didn't know the father of the baby? No. That so wasn't her. And anyone who knew her would realize it was a lie.

That left her with refusing to divulge the father's name, saying he wanted nothing to do with her or the baby. But was that how Luca would truly feel? Would he turn his back on them both and walk away?

The Luca she'd known all these years would never do such a thing. No, he would stand by her out of obligation. But how would that work? She would make him miserable, and vice versa. Talk about a mess.

Elena switched into a dressy pair of shorts and a cotton top. She stopped in front of the mirror and decided to pull her hair up into a ponytail. She couldn't believe that in the midst of everything she was going on a picnic with Luca.

Five minutes later, she returned to find her mother and Luca deep in conversation about Annabelle's fiancé. They both stopped talking and turned to her.

"I'm ready," Elena said.

"Are you feeling better now?" Her mother sent her a concerned look.

"Yes. You're the one who needs to take it easy. I feel really bad about leaving you again."

"Nonsense. I'll be fine." Her mother smiled.

She and Luca said goodbye to her mother and headed outside. Once the door was shut, Elena said, "Sorry about that. You know how my mother can be."

"So there's nothing to her worries?"

Drat. Now wasn't the time to get into her pregnancy. It would wait until the end of the week, just like she'd planned. "No. I am not sick. I promise."

Luca arched a brow. "But something is wrong. I can feel it. Are you sure you're up for the picnic?"

She nodded. "It sounds like a lot of fun."

He paused as though evaluating her sincerity. "I still can't believe my sister is taking this long walk down memory lane with all these activities that we did when we were kids."

"I think it's sweet. She gets to share a bit of her past with her fiancé, and it's a way of saying goodbye to that part of her life before she sets out on a new journey."

Luca's smile broadened. "You got all that out of my sister's invitation?"

Elena nodded. "I think it's quite original and a lot of fun. Has she said what she's planning for the wedding?"

"She said the engagement is the fun part and her wedding will be formal. The best part, she said, will be the honeymoon."

"I like the way your sister thinks."

"And how about you?" Luca asked. "Have you met anyone special?"

"No." The answer came out too quickly and too vehemently. She inwardly groaned. "You know how it is with work and traveling. I hardly have a minute to myself."

Luca's inquisitive gaze was full of questions. "Is that the only reason?"

He was referring to their night together. She wasn't about to let him know that it had meant more to her than it should have. "Of course."

He nodded and looked away.

And then she knew exactly how to jerk him out of this train of thought. "The way you're questioning me, I'm starting to think you've been spending too much time with my mother."

"Ouch. That bad, huh?"

She smiled and nodded. "I'd rather talk about this picnic."

"Someone in your line of work probably doesn't eat much."

"Oh, come on. You know me. I love food."

He gave her an appraising look. "You sure don't look like it. You have all of the curves in just the right places."

A tentative smile pulled at her lips. "Well, thank you. I think. I'm just fortunate that I have a really fast metabolism, because there's hardly a thing I don't like."

He didn't say anything. They continued to walk along the dirt path to the bluff, and the silence dragged on. So much for their conversation.

She glanced over at Luca. She was surprised he hadn't chastised her for disappearing on him last night. Perhaps that was why he'd grown quiet.

"It's a beautiful day," she said, trying to break the tension.

He glanced up from where he'd been studying the ground. "Uh, yes, it is."

"Your sister seems to be having a good time this week."

"Uh-huh."

"I haven't been on a picnic since I was a kid."

"Uh-huh."

She doubted he'd heard a word she'd said. "I was thinking of cutting all my hair off."

"That's good."

She wondered what he'd say to this. "I'm thinking of dyeing it purple."

"Wait." Luca stopped walking and looked at her. "Did you say you're dyeing your hair purple?"

She smiled and nodded. "Wondered if you'd notice."

It was then that she realized she was smiling. That was something she hadn't done in what felt like forever. Her life had taken so many twists and turns in the past couple of months that she'd forgotten what it was like to unwind and enjoy the sunshine on her face and breathe in the sea air.

"I'd certainly notice something like that." Then concern filled Luca's eyes. "Please tell me you're joking."

She wasn't quite ready to quit teasing him. "I don't know. It'd certainly be different."

"Trust me, you don't have to go to those lengths to be unique."

She wasn't sure she liked that comment. "What exactly does that mean?"

He held up his hands as though to fend her off. "No offense meant. I was just referring to the way you left Mirraccino and made a name for yourself. Not many people achieve such notable accomplishments."

"You act like that's such a big deal. It's not like I'm an earl."

"I was born into that title. It had nothing to do with me. You, on the other hand, worked hard and earned a prestigious place as the face of the famous Lauren Renard line."

His words meant a lot to her—more than she'd expected. "Thank you."

Luca reached out, grabbing her hand. When she stopped walking and turned to him, he said, "Listen, I know I really messed things up in Paris, and I'm sorry. I don't want to lose our friendship."

With all her heart, she wanted to believe him—believe that their friendship was strong enough to overcome any obstacle. But that night had changed everything. And how would he feel toward her once he learned she was carrying his child?

She pulled her hand away. "Things are different now. We're not kids anymore."

"What's that supposed to mean? Are you saying you never want to see me again?"

"It means…" In that moment, she got choked up. She glanced away, not wanting Luca to see the unshed tears in her eyes. Darn pregnancy hormones. "I can't do this. Not here. Not now."

He placed a hand beneath her chin and lifted until their gazes met. In his eyes, she saw strength, but more than that, she saw tenderness and warmth. She latched on to that and found that between his touch and his gaze, her rising emotions had calmed.

Being this close to him had her remembering their brief Paris affair. Her gaze dipped to Luca's mouth—to his very tempting lips. What would he do if she leaned forward and pressed her mouth to his?

As if in answer, he turned away and started walking.

She stifled a sigh. If only things were different.

She rushed to catch up to him. The truth was in this particular moment, she didn't trust him. He'd said and done things with her in Paris that he now wanted to conveniently sweep under the rug. Was that how he'd feel about this supposed friendship once he found out they were to be linked for life?

She didn't know what to believe. She'd thought she'd known Steven, and she'd been horribly wrong about him. Now she didn't trust herself to make good decisions where men were concerned.

If he'd known she had been considering kissing him back there, he didn't let on. And that was fine by her. She'd had a moment of weakness. It wouldn't happen again.

CHAPTER FIVE

WHAT WAS GOING on with Elena?

Nothing had been the same since they made love. And he was left feeling—feeling…ugh! He didn't know how he felt, except confused and frustrated.

The rising sound of excited voices drew his attention. Today's guests consisted of the same group from dinner the prior evening minus the twin princes and their spouses. They all had prior engagements that they couldn't cancel. His sister took it all in stride. That was one thing Luca admired about his sister, her ability to handle the curves life threw her way with a minimum of fuss.

He wished he could be that way around Elena, but she got under his skin. She made him experience emotions he didn't want to feel and provoked him to act out of character. No one had ever had that sort of effect on him.

It was then that Luca noticed she was speaking with Alec, Luca's cousin. She smiled and toyed with her ponytail as it fell down over her shoulder. She was engaging and charming with his cousin. The thought of her being drawn into Alec's arms had Luca's jaw tightening. What was up with that?

The scene unfolding before him shouldn't bother him. After all, this was what he wanted, wasn't it? It wasn't like he wanted to romance Elena. The night they'd shared had been a mistake. Nothing more.

He turned away, refusing to keep watching. What Elena chose to do and whom she chose to do it with was absolutely none of his business.

He made his way over to his future brother-in-law, Grayson Landers. Luca was pleasantly surprised and relieved to find his little sister had chosen a really good guy. As they talked about Grayson's growing cybercafé business, Luca found himself periodically gazing in Elena's direction. She'd seemed to relax and unwind now that she'd moved away from him. The thought slugged him in the gut.

With lunch cleared, Annabelle let them know that it was time for games. A large white tent and a gentle breeze offset the warmth of the sun. But it was the heat he experienced when he was close to Elena that worried him. So when the guests set aside their hard lemonade and iced tea sangrias in order to play badminton, Luca made sure he played the opposite side of the net from Elena. And when it was time for bocce ball, he stood in the background sipping on a tall glass of ice water.

He had to keep all his wits about him, because something had happened back in that field—something intense had coursed between him and Elena. And it wasn't good. He knew what it was like to hold her in his arms, and now he wanted more. It wasn't logical. It wasn't realistic. But the desire was there every time they were within each other's orbits.

But even if she did want him, he could never be the sort of man she needed. He just couldn't commit himself to a lifetime of unhappiness. He'd watched it with his parents. They put on a good show for people, but they were very different behind closed doors. He forced away the memories of the secret arguments he had overheard as a child.

Annabelle had been too young to have noticed these things or else she didn't want to acknowledge that their parents' marriage had been far from perfect. And Luca had no intention of changing that for her. Their mother's murder had devastated both of them. Whatever comfort Annabelle found in her memories of their family, she deserved. They'd all endured far too much for one lifetime.

Once the badminton and bocce wound down, Annabelle

clinked a butter knife against her lemonade glass. Silence fell over the small group. "Okay. Everyone gather round."

Luca had an uneasy feeling as he took a seat at the large round table. His sister was up to something because she had a mischievous smile on her face. Every time she looked that way, he knew he was in trouble. It was just then that Elena drew a chair up next to his.

"Are you having a good time?" He didn't know why he'd asked. It wasn't like he really wanted to know if she was enjoying his cousin's company more than his.

She nodded. "Surprisingly, I am."

Annabelle again clinked her glass with her butter knife. She waited until she had everyone's attention. "I hope you all are having as much fun as I am. Thank you for joining in the celebration this week. And now it's time for a blast from the past."

The impish expression had yet to leave his sister's face, making Luca even more concerned at what she might be up to. Past experience told him he wasn't going to like it. He braced himself for what she said next.

She picked up an empty wine bottle and placed it on its side in the middle of the table. "Remember this?"

Remember what? Where was Annabelle going with this? He turned a questioning gaze to Elena. Her eyes widened, and then she turned a worried look his way. His gut knotted up tight.

"I can tell by the puzzled look on my brother's face that he doesn't have a clue." She looked directly at him. There was a gleam of devilment in her eyes. He was doomed. She continued, "It's called spin the bottle, Luca. Except that my version is a mix between spin the bottle and truth or dare."

His sister was always one to be creative with the rules. That was probably how she got herself in serious trouble with a killer. Thank goodness Grayson had been there.

The thought of his sister facing down their mother's killer shook Luca to the core.

And then guilt settled in. He should have been there to protect her—not that his sister ever needed anyone to play hero. She had a stubborn and independent streak, just like their mother. But that didn't lessen his guilt for not being there—for not uncovering the killer himself. Perhaps he had been gone far too long.

But now that he'd spoken with his father, things were changing. If all worked out, he would be around more for his family. But that didn't mean he had to stick around for this walk down memory lane.

He knew exactly how his sister would play the game— she would make people squirm. And he wasn't having any part of it. He started to get up to leave when Elena reached out, placing her hand on his arm.

She leaned over and whispered, "Please don't go."

His body tensed as he was torn between leaving before this day went horribly sideways and doing as Elena asked. It wasn't like he owed Elena anything. In all honesty, he wasn't even her official escort. He'd merely walked with her to the picnic. He knew he was just making up excuses in order to leave without a guilty conscience.

Then his gaze lifted and met Elena's. The worry was still there. No. It was panic. Why was she so upset about the game? Then again, who was he to question her when all he wanted was out of there?

He leaned toward her. It was then that a gentle breeze picked up and with it carried the not-too-sweet scent of jasmine perfume. He inhaled a little deeper. Every time he smelled that scent, he thought of Elena. She'd started wearing that perfume as a teenager. For some reason, he'd thought now that she was a famous model she'd have switched to a more trendy fragrance. Was it possible that everything about her hadn't changed?

And then, remembering he was supposed to say something, he whispered in her ear, "Come with me."

"I can't leave your sister's party."

"Sure you can. Come on."

"Luca, be serious. Everyone will notice."

He knew she was right, but that didn't mean he wanted to sit here and play a child's game. "I don't want to do this."

Elena squeezed his hand. "It'll be all right."

His fingers instinctively wrapped around hers. It was such a simple act, and yet his heart was racing. He loved the feel of her hand in his. His thumb stroked the back of her hand.

And then he remembered that they weren't alone. They had an audience that included his very astute sister. Thankfully the table and the white linen tablecloth hid their clasped hands from view. But not wanting to take any chances, he forced himself to release Elena's hand.

"Since I'm the bride, I'll go first." Annabelle smiled as she gazed directly at Luca.

He resisted the urge to shift in his seat. He would not be outmaneuvered by his little sister, and especially not over some childish game.

Annabelle spun the bottle. It circled round and round. Each time it neared him, the breath caught in his lungs. And then it started to slow down. His body tensed.

Thankfully the bottle didn't point at him. But it did point to Elena. He glanced her way, and she looked as pale as a ghost. Oh, no. This wasn't good. He wanted to tell her that she should have listened to him when he suggested they leave together, but he resisted.

Annabelle beamed. That was never a good sign. He wanted to speak up and tell his sister to back off, but before he could utter a word, his sister said, "Okay, Elena, you're first. Truth? Or dare?"

Elena looked horrified that she'd just been caught in his sister's crosshairs.

Luca leaned forward. "Annabelle, I don't think this is a good idea."

That was probably the wrong thing to say. His sister's eyes lit up. "Oh, come on, Luca. Loosen up." Everyone's gaze moved back to Elena. Once again his sister said, "Truth? Or dare?"

A moment passed as everyone waited for Elena to decide.

"Dare," she said so softly that Luca wasn't sure what she'd actually said.

"What was that?" Annabelle asked.

"Dare," Elena said louder.

Annabelle pressed her lips together as she made a show of making up her mind. She was having too much fun with this. Her gaze moved back and forth between him and Elena. What was she thinking? Surely she wouldn't—

"I dare you to kiss my brother."

Elena's mouth gaped, but nothing came out.

"Annabelle, enough is enough," Luca said.

"Tsk, tsk, brother." His sister shook her finger at him. "Since when did you become the serious one? I thought you enjoyed fun and games."

"But this is different—"

"Really? How so?"

He could feel all eyes on him now. What had he done? Was everyone going to guess that he had a thing for Elena?

Before he could find a way out of this mess, Elena leaned toward him. She grabbed the front of his shirt and pulled him toward her. What in the world?

The next thing he knew, Elena's lips were pressed to his. They were warm and so very sweet. His eyes drifted shut as a moan swelled in the back of his throat. Did she know how excruciating this was for him? Did she know how many sleepless nights he'd spent thinking of their lovemaking?

Remembering that they had an audience, he squelched the moan. It took all of his self-restraint to keep his hands to himself. He longed to crush Elena to him. He ached to feel her body next to him with their hearts beating in unison.

If they were alone, he'd kiss her slowly and gently at first. He'd let the hunger and desire build. And just when neither of them could take it anymore, he'd deepen the kiss. Just like before...

They'd been so good together.

It was like they'd been made for each other.

A moan started low and grew. Oh, yeah, her kisses were as sweet as berries and held the promise of so much more. If he were to pull her closer—

Elena pulled back.

And as quickly as the kiss began, it ended. His eyes opened to find her frowning at him. It would appear he'd lost his touch, and along with it he'd lost any semblance of a good mood.

CHAPTER SIX

"ELENA, WAIT!"

She didn't stop. She didn't slow down. In fact, Elena made a point of picking up her pace. The last thing she wanted to do now was deal with Luca.

She'd forced herself to remain at the party until it was over, but she'd made sure to keep her distance from Luca. She didn't trust herself around him. That kiss had reminded her of their night together. And that wasn't good. She had to keep her wits about her.

Steven and Luca weren't the first men in her life who had said sweet nothings to sway her to let her guard down. The others had been photographers, models and other men in the fashion industry. She'd done well navigating her way between the truth and the lies—until Steven.

She'd thought she'd known Steven. He'd seemed so sweet and charming when she'd met him in the Paris café. When she'd dropped her phone, he'd picked it up for her. A bit of casual chitchat led to him asking her to join him for a cup of coffee. From there they'd had dinner. To say it was a whirlwind relationship was putting it mildly. Maybe that was why she'd held back. Maybe there was something in the back of her mind that had said it was all too easy.

She wasn't used to things coming to her easily. Sure, she'd been raised on the royal estate of Mirraccino. But she was raised as an employee's child—someone who was forced to keep to the shadows. When there were grand functions, she had watched them from afar. She'd never had any illusions that she was anything but the help's daughter—a nobody.

When she'd moved to Paris, there was no modeling job waiting for her. She'd waitressed until she had enough money to have a portfolio made and then she started making the rounds of the modeling agencies. No part of her journey had been handed to her. But she'd never regretted any of it. She'd learned a lot and grown as a person.

So when Steven seemed more than willing to let their relationship escalate quickly, she'd put on the brakes. He'd been dropping hints about the future—their future. It had all been happening too easily—and too fast.

When their photo had been taken by an investigator his wife had hired, the whole truth about Steven came out. They had been caught kissing near the Arc de Triomphe, but luckily that was all they'd done. It was what she'd told Steven's wife when the irate woman had confronted her. No matter what Elena said, the woman refused to believe that it was a kiss and nothing more.

Elena had tried to explain how Steven had lied to her about himself and hidden the fact that he was already married. His family had conveniently been on vacation in Australia visiting his in-laws while he'd been sweet-talking Elena.

By the time Luca had arrived in Paris, Elena had been at her lowest. And Luca had been so vulnerable—so open. She'd let her guard down—perhaps too much. Obviously too much, or she wouldn't be pregnant.

She inwardly groaned. She shouldn't have chosen the dare. She could still feel Luca's lips on hers. She knew how easily his kisses could make her forget her common sense. The events of that night came crashing back to her. And the part that stuck out the most was how their night in Paris had all started with a single kiss.

And look where it'd landed them. But of course Luca didn't know yet. She was trying so hard to keep everything light and fun until the week was out, but at every turn Luca was making that increasingly difficult. Just like now. Couldn't he just let her go? Didn't he understand that she needed some alone time?

His fingers reached out, touching her shoulder. "Hey, slow down. What is this, a race?"

She came to an abrupt halt. She spun around and faced him. "What was that kiss back there?"

"A dare issued by my sister." He paused. Suddenly his eyes widened. "You surely don't think I put her up to it, do you?"

Elena crossed her arms. "I'm not sure what to think."

"Sure you do. We're still best friends. Just like always."

"Not like always. Things have changed."

"You keep saying that, but we don't have to let one night ruin a lifetime of friendship." His eyes pleaded with her.

"Why don't you understand that the bell can't be un-rung?"

"I think you're making too much of things."

"Really? Then how would you explain that kiss?"

"What about it? It was a dare. A game. No big deal."

"This is me you're talking to," Elena said. "You can't lie to me. I was on the other end of that kiss, and you kissed me back."

He shook his head, not wanting to admit that there was something going on between them. "You're making too much of it."

"And you're working too hard to deny there was something to that kiss. Now why would that be?"

He ran a hand over the scruff lining his chiseled jaw. "It must just have been instinctive. After all, I'm not used to women literally throwing themselves at me."

Elena sighed. "Well, your sister saw that the kiss was more than a friendly peck. You know she's going to make something of it."

"Not if we don't let her."

Nervous laughter escaped her lips. "Have you met your

sister? No one tells her what to do, and that includes her big brother."

Luca's lips settled into a firm line. Apparently he didn't find it amusing. She didn't blame him. This whole thing was getting sticky. Maybe she should just fess up now about the baby.

But what did she say? Did she just blurt it out? No. It had to be handled delicately.

"Luca—"

"Elena—"

They both spoke at once. Both surprised, they stopped and stared at each other.

"Ladies go first." Luca looked at her expectantly.

Suddenly her nerve failed her. She needed more time. She had to think of the right words. "You go first. You look like you have something important to say."

He glanced at his phone. "I have to get to a meeting with Prince Demetrius."

"Oh." She noticed how he used the word *meeting*. "Do you two have business together?"

"I hope so." Then a guilty look came over his face. "Would it be all right if I left you here?"

"Seriously? You're worried about me walking home alone in broad daylight while on the royal estate—"

"Okay. Okay. I get the point. I just didn't want you to think that I was ditching you."

"I'll be fine. Go have your meeting. I hope it goes well."

He started to walk back to the palace, but then he turned back to her. "What was it you wanted to tell me?"

"It can wait."

"You're sure?"

"Positive." What they needed to discuss was going to take much longer than the couple of minutes that he had right now. And she was certain he wouldn't be able to think clearly after she told him. "We'll catch up later."

"You can count on it. Wish me luck."

"Good luck."

And with that he was gone. She was left to wonder what business he had with the crown prince. The last she knew Luca was into investments or some such thing, but what would that have to do with Mirraccino? And the last time they'd discussed his profession, he'd sworn her to secrecy until he told his father. So what exactly was he up to?

"I'm sorry—I can't help."

Luca stared at the crown prince, wishing he'd heard him incorrectly. This couldn't be right. He knew for a fact that Mirraccino was flourishing. So why was his cousin turning down his business plan?

"If it's the price," Luca said, "I'm sure we can negotiate it."

The truth of the matter was that he hadn't had near enough time to formulate any solid numbers. But the crown prince's schedule was kept quiet due to security concerns, and Luca didn't want to miss a chance to talk with him in person. His cousin was being groomed to take over the throne. And though Demetrius traveled often for diplomatic duties, he was also making business connections to keep Mirraccino flourishing.

Demetrius barely took his eyes off his young daughter. She was a toddler now, with a rosy smile just like her mother. She was into everything and getting faster on her toes each day. "It's not the price." When Princess Katrina landed on her diapered backside, Demetrius offered his hands for her to cling to while she got back on her feet. "This is just a really bad time. Perhaps we can revisit this in six months or a year?"

Luca had examined enough of the business's records to know there wouldn't be a lemon grove in six months, much less a year. It needed a large infusion of cash as of yesterday. But he refused to give up. If he hadn't let his ego rule his common sense, he would have returned to his home in Halencia long before now. He would have known the condition of his family's business.

"Perhaps I could speak with the king," Luca said.

"No." Demetrius frowned. Obviously he wasn't used to people not accepting the finality of his word. "My father is not seeing anyone."

Luca had noticed the king's absence since he'd arrived at the palace, but he'd thought his uncle was just feeling under the weather. "Is he okay?"

"I really don't want to discuss my father."

Princess Katrina toppled over on her backside once more, but this time she didn't laugh it off. She started slowly with a couple of unhappy grunts before it grew into a full-on cry. Demetrius immediately swung her little body up into his arms. "Is someone ready for a nap?" He shushed her before looking back at Luca. "I really am sorry. Now, I need to get this princess to her crib."

Luca watched the crown prince walk away. All the while Demetrius talked in soft, gentle tones that seemed to soothe his daughter. Luca wanted to be upset with him for immediately turning down his proposal without an explanation, but it was so hard to be angry with a man holding a baby in his arms.

Luca shook his head as he went to stand next to the elongated library window. He stared off into the clear blue sky. He couldn't imagine dividing his life between family and business. That was exactly what he'd been avoiding all this time—the complications.

He was so much better off alone.

CHAPTER SEVEN

THIS IS IT.

Today is the day.

Elena had awoken just as the sun rose the next morning. She hadn't slept well. Her thoughts wouldn't slow down enough for her to sleep more than an hour or two at a time. Finally she gave up.

By the time she stepped out of bed, she'd accepted that party or no party, she had to tell Luca about the baby. Keeping this secret was eating her up inside. They'd never kept secrets from each other until now. And this wasn't just any secret—it was gigantic and life changing.

She knew Luca had no intention of settling down with a family—ever. He said that families were too complicated and that love didn't last. She felt sorry for him. A lifetime was a long time to be alone.

She might have given romance a try and failed miserably, but at least she'd put herself out there. It bothered her that Luca wouldn't even try. What did that mean for their child? Would Luca insist on keeping their son or daughter at arm's length?

Elena hoped Luca would make an exception for his own flesh and blood. But he hadn't for his father or sister. Elena inwardly groaned. She'd been going in these endless circles all night. The only way to get some real answers was to speak to Luca.

After showering and dressing, she went downstairs to check on her mother. Elena found her in the kitchen about to prepare food for her invited guests. It appeared that Wednesday involved another card game.

Elena had her mother sit at the kitchen table while Elena set to work preparing a meat and cheese platter as well as a fruit and vegetable one. The whole time her mother filled her in on friends and family, who had married and who was expecting babies. Elena got the hint. Her mother was anxious to expand the family. She wondered what her mother would think if she knew the truth about Elena's condition.

"Are you sure I can't do anything else?" Elena asked as she placed the last platter in the fridge.

"No. You've done plenty by preparing lunch for everyone. Now, don't you have something to do this afternoon?"

"Mother, are you trying to get rid of me?" She eyed her mother, who suddenly looked flustered.

"Of course not. I'm not trying to get rid of you. It's just that there are four of us already. You would be a fifth person, and that wouldn't work well for cards."

"Okay." Something told her there was more to her mother shoving her out the door than setting her card game off balance. "Well, I should be going soon."

"Is Luca coming to pick you up?"

Elena rinsed off her hands in the kitchen sink. "Not that I know of." Of all the days she would welcome him picking her up, this would be the day he would skip out on her. "But I'm sure I'll run into him at the party. Unless, of course, you want me to stay home. I know you already have a foursome for cards, but I could take care of the food and clean up."

"That's sweet of you." Her mother reached out and patted Elena's arm. "But not necessary. You just go and have a good time."

Elena didn't know if she'd have a good time. Most likely it would not be a good day, but it was like her father taught her about peeling off a bandage—the faster you did it, the sooner the pain ended. Now it was time to yank off a very big bandage.

"I just need to get ready." Elena had changed outfits about a half dozen times. She couldn't tell if it was her imagination or not, but her clothes were starting to get snug—not that they'd been loose in the first place.

Elena glanced down at her stylish white cotton tank top, jean shorts and flip-flops with blue and white bows. The invitation had said casual dress. Maybe this was too casual.

Which meant once again rooting through her closet to put together just the right outfit—one that was casual but not too casual, dressy but not too dressy, and something that was comfortable, but again, not too comfortable.

"I'll be right back." Elena headed for the steps to the second story.

Twenty minutes later, she stared in the mirror at the coral sundress. It was actually one of the first designs she'd done. Designer Francois Lacroix had told her that she not only had to sketch her ideas but she also had to bring them to life. It wasn't frilly. It had a simple neckline with a beaded bodice that fit snugly. It was gathered just below the bodice and an embroidered hemline landed just above her knees.

She smoothed her hands over her midsection. She'd swear that she'd put on weight, but the scale in the bathroom said she hadn't gained an ounce. She turned to the side and puffed out her stomach, wondering what she'd look like months from now. They said your bustline expanded. She was looking forward to that part. Maybe then she'd be more than a padded B cup.

Everything about this pregnancy intrigued her, almost as much as all the unknowns and the forthcoming pain scared her. It might be easier if she had someone to go through it with her. Luca's handsome face came to mind, but she immediately dismissed it. He'd made it perfectly clear that he had no interest in extending his family line—title or no title. She'd never imagined that she'd end up a single mother, but sometimes you had to play the cards life dealt you—

"Elena! Elena, get down here." Her mother's voice was filled with urgency.

Oh, no! Elena rushed for the steps. Her mother must have reinjured herself. Elena had told her that she was doing too much, but her mother would not listen.

Elena almost missed the last step on the way down, but luckily she had her hand on the banister and was able to regain her balance. She rushed into the living room, where her mother was sitting in her favorite armchair.

"What's the matter?" Elena pressed a hand to her pounding chest.

Her mother's face was creased with frown lines. "This!" She turned the digital tablet Elena had gotten her for Christmas so Elena could see it. "Here. Take it. I can't look at it any longer. What are we going to do?"

Whatever her mother was going on about couldn't be nearly as bad as she was making it out to be. Her mother always did have a bit of an air for the dramatic. Elena took the tablet and gazed at the picture filling the screen.

It was an image of her...and Steven.

Elena's stomach plummeted down to her bare feet.

How could this be? They'd ended things the same day this picture was taken. She remembered wearing that exact outfit. This must be one of the photos the investigator had taken of them.

"Tell me it isn't true," her mother pleaded. "You'd never get involved with a married man. Right?" When Elena didn't say anything, her mother nervously chattered on. "I told your father that nothing good would come of you going so far from home. And now this. Well, what do you have to say for yourself?"

"Mother, I can't think when you keep going on like that. Just give me a second."

Her mother sighed but quieted down.

Elena scrolled down past the damning photo that was on a very popular tabloid website. The headlines read:

From Model to Home Wrecker!
Banking CEO Caught in Lover's Arms!
That Kiss Is Going to Cost Him Millions!

Elena's gaze stuck on the headlines as anger and humiliation churned within her. She forced herself to read the attached article. Word by painful word she choked down the lies and innuendo.

And the worst part was the press made it seem like that picture was new. It was more than two months old. She hadn't seen, much less talked to, Steven in that time. Nor did she intend to ever speak to him again. She'd been a victim here, but the press made it sound like she was a willing accomplice. She hadn't even known he was married. He'd conveniently forgotten to mention that part.

This was a disaster!

And it wasn't just her reputation that was on the line. It was going to affect her job, as her contract contained a morality clause. And when the paparazzi found out she was pregnant, they were going to jump to the wrong conclusion. It was like her life was a series of dominoes and now that the first one had fallen, the rest would follow. And it would end with Luca.

Luca!

She'd thought there would be time to speak with him. She'd thought she could break the news of her pregnancy to him gently. And now her best-laid plans were ruined. She had to get to him before he read these blatant lies.

"Well," her mother prompted, "what do you have to say for yourself?"

"I have to go." Elena turned to find her purse. She needed her phone. She had to call him. Had to warn him about the firestorm that was headed her way—and in turn their innocent baby's way.

"Go?" Her mother's voice rose to a screechy level. "Go where? We have to talk."

"I have something I need to do." Where was her purse? It had to be around here somewhere. She scanned the couch and the chairs in the living room. It wasn't there. *Think. Where did you leave it?*

Her thoughts were muddled and her pulse was racing. She was certain that all this stress wasn't good for the baby, but she wouldn't be able to calm down until she spoke with Luca.

She rushed to the kitchen. A quick scan of the house turned up her purse on the counter, where she'd placed it before preparing lunch for her mother and her friends.

"Elena, stop. You can't just rush out of here." Her mother balanced herself on her crutches in the doorway.

Elena paused at the front door to slip on her shoes. "I'm going. And you aren't going to stop me." Then, realizing that her mother was worried about her, she added, "Just concentrate on your card game. Don't worry about this. I have everything under control."

Her mother's face crumpled. Was she going to cry?

Elena hugged her mother. "I made a mistake. A huge mistake, and now it's coming back to bite me in a really big way. But it's not like the press is making out."

"Thank goodness. What can I do to help?"

"Forget you ever read that batch of lies." With her purse and phone in hand, she opened the front door. "I have something very important to do. Will you be all right?"

Her mother nodded. "Go ahead. I'm fine."

Elena rushed out the door and didn't slow down. She was a woman on a mission. She needed to speak to Luca before he read the headlines. Before he jumped to the wrong conclusion like the rest of the world.

Her fingers trembled as she reached for her phone. The display showed that she had three missed calls—all from

Lauren Renard. Elena's stomach knotted. The story was already making the rounds in short order. But Lauren would have to wait.

Right now, Elena's priority was Luca. She sought out his number on her phone. It rang once and went to voice mail. She disconnected and tried again. Once more, she was forwarded to his voice mail. She groaned inwardly.

"Luca, it's Elena. Call me when you get this message. It's important."

She disconnected the call. Where was he? And why did he have his calls forwarded to his voice mail today, of all days?

She could only hope he attended today's festivities. The invitation hadn't said what was planned for the day. It was going to be a surprise. Elena had to admit that initially she'd been quite intrigued with the mystery.

So far Annabelle had taken them on a fun trip down memory lane. Except for yesterday's spin the bottle game, Elena had enjoyed herself. Just the mere thought of that kiss yesterday sent heat rushing to her cheeks. She wondered if Annabelle was on to them.

Elena was still thinking all this over when she arrived at the far side of the palace. Before her stood a carnival, just like the ones they'd visited as kids. There was a Ferris wheel, game booths and food vendors. It was…it was amazing. Too bad she wouldn't get to enjoy any of it.

She walked around the small carnival, but she still hadn't spotted Luca. She couldn't imagine he'd miss it, not after he'd made the point that his attendance was mandatory.

"Elena, there you are." Annabelle and Grayson approached her. Annabelle wore a gleeful smile while holding cotton candy in her hand. "What do you think?"

It took Elena a moment to realize Annabelle was referring to the party and not to the nasty piece of gossip on the internet. "I think you've outdone yourself." Elena forced a smile on her face. "This entire week has been amazing."

"And it's not over yet." Annabelle reached for her fiancé's hand.

Elena did her best to act normal. "You're very lucky to have found someone so wonderful."

Annabelle blushed. "I know. Don't ask me how close I came to losing him."

"That wouldn't have happened." Grayson stared into Annabelle's eyes. "I know when I have a good thing. And you're the best."

"Aw…" Annabelle turned into his arms. She lifted on her tiptoes and pressed her lips to his.

Elena turned to walk away and leave the lovebirds alone—or as alone as they could be in the middle of a carnival. She really needed to find Luca.

"Elena, did you happen to see my brother?" Annabelle called out.

Elena turned back. "Actually, I was looking for him. I thought he would be here."

"I did, too, but he was distracted last night. He didn't even come down to dinner."

Oh, no. Had he heard something? Did he already know that she'd made a fool of herself in front of the whole world?

"So you haven't spoken to him since yesterday?"

Annabelle shook her head. "I wouldn't worry. It probably has something to do with my father arriving yesterday. Those two can get on each other's nerves."

"Well, if you see him, can you tell him that I'm looking for him?"

"I will. But before you go, I want to ask you something." Annabelle's expression grew serious.

"Um, sure. What do you need?"

"I, well, we wanted to know if you'd be in our wedding?"

"You want me to stand up for you?"

Annabelle smiled and nodded. "I know you're really busy now that you're a world-famous model, but the wedding is almost a year out. Please say that you'll do it. I know Luca would like it. A lot."

Elena wasn't so sure how to take Annabelle's last comment, so she just let it slide. "I'd be honored. Thank you for asking me."

Annabelle turned a triumphant look to Grayson. "I told you she'd do it. This wedding is starting to come together."

"I know it's going to be just as fabulous as your engagement," Elena said.

"Just not as fun," Grayson said.

"You'll just have to wait for the honeymoon." Annabelle sent him a devilish look.

Just then a man in a dark suit and sunglasses strode toward them. Elena guessed he was part of the palace security. She hoped nothing was wrong. But seeing as the man would want to speak with Annabelle, the king's niece, Elena was ready to make a quick exit.

"Looks like someone is searching for you." Elena pointed out the man.

"Oh." Annabelle frowned. "And here everything was going so well. I should have known it was too good to be true."

"Don't worry." Grayson rubbed his fiancée's shoulders. "Whatever it is, we'll get it straightened out and get back to the celebration."

Annabelle sent Grayson a worried look. "I hope so."

"I'll let you deal with it." Elena started to walk away.

"Ms. Ricci, could I speak to you?"

Elena paused at the sound of her name. An uneasy feeling inched down her spine. With great trepidation she turned to the man. "Yes?"

Out of the corner of her eye, she could see the surprised

look on Annabelle's face. Elena wondered if she was wearing a similar expression.

"Excuse me, ma'am. I was informed that you would be here."

"What can I do for you?"

"Ma'am, there are a bunch of reporters at the gate demanding to speak with you. What should we do?"

It felt as though the bottom had fallen out of her world. The article had just made the tabloid that morning and they were already seeking her out. She wondered what other information they had. She was certain that none of it would be good news.

"Did they say what they wanted?"

"No, ma'am."

Annabelle stepped up then. "Tell them to go away. Elena is my guest today, and she doesn't want to be hounded by the press."

"Yes, ma'am." The security guard pulled out his phone as he started to walk away.

"What do you think that's all about?" Annabelle asked.

"I…I have a confession." Elena's gaze dropped to the ground.

"That sounds awfully dire. Surely it can't be that bad."

Elena shrugged. "I guess it depends on how you look at it."

"I think I should go get another drink," Grayson said and slipped away.

"You don't have to tell me," Annabelle said.

"I do." Elena was so tired of keeping secrets. "There's a story in a tabloid and a photo linking me with a married man."

Annabelle's perfectly plucked brows rose, but she didn't say anything.

"It's not true. At least not like they are saying. I didn't

know he was married. He conveniently left that part out when we met. And it's been over for a while now."

Annabelle reached out and squeezed her arm. "It's okay. We've all made mistakes, but the paparazzi doesn't care about those mistakes unless you're an international public figure. I have a feeling this won't be your last time in the tabloids."

"I'd totally understand if you want me to go now. I don't want to ruin your party."

"Nonsense. You have to stay. We aren't going to let the paparazzi ruin our day."

"I don't think I'll ever get used to them."

"Me, either. We just have to stick together."

"Thanks for being so understanding." They shared a quick hug and then Elena said, "I think I'll go get a drink. It's a little warm out here today."

She moved away and spotted a lemonade stand. No doubt they'd used lemons from the DiSalvo lemon grove. They were the best. And she was thirsty. Hunting for Luca in the bright sunshine had her parched. And she didn't know where else to look for him…unless she was to search the palace. However, she doubted security was going to let that happen.

She stood in line for the lemonade. It seemed to be a popular stand. And she couldn't blame them. This was the best lemonade in the world. Not too sweet. Not too tart. It was just perfect. And any other day, she'd be excited to have some, but not today. Today she needed to find Luca before he stumbled across the lies and innuendos.

Once she had her refreshment in hand, she peered all around. He had to be here somewhere. But she couldn't spot him. She pulled out her phone and tried his cell. Again, it went to voice mail.

She'd just slipped the phone into her purse when she heard, "Elena, there you are."

She turned to find Luca approaching her. He was dressed casually in white shorts and a blue collared shirt with the sleeves rolled up. And she'd never seen him look more handsome. Of course, it helped that he was smiling right at her. He was like the sun, parting her clouds of gloom and doom.

He stepped up to her. "We need to talk."

"I know."

"You do?" Luca asked with a puzzled look on his face.

"Sorry. I thought you wanted to tell me about the press at the front gate."

He arched a dark brow. "No, but what are they doing here?"

She waved off his question, hoping he wouldn't make a big deal out of it. "It's nothing. We sent them away."

"We?"

"Your sister was here when one of the security guards stopped by. She instructed him to send the reporters away." And before he could question her further about the paparazzi, she asked, "So what did you want to talk to me about?"

Luca glanced around at the colorful tents. "It can wait until I win you a teddy bear at the ball toss."

So he really didn't know about the tabloid story. The breath that she didn't realize she'd been holding whooshed from her lungs. In actuality, she wasn't sure if this news made things better or worse for her. On second thought, it didn't do either. It just delayed the inevitable.

And then he paused and looked at her. She found herself staring into his blue-gray eyes. Some days they were bluer, but today they were a deeper gray. He had something on his mind. Just wait until he heard what she had to tell him. His eyes would turn dark and stormy.

"Elena, why are you frowning at me? I know I'm late to

the festivities, but you don't have to look that upset. What happened to bring the paparazzi here?"

She glanced around at all of the people they knew. This definitely wasn't the place to give him life-altering news. "I can't talk about it. Not here."

"Elena, there is obviously a problem. So out with it."

Just then her phone rang. She didn't even have to look at the caller ID to know it was Lauren again. She'd never called this many times in a row. With each phone call, Elena's hope of salvaging her job diminished.

"Do you need to get that?"

She shook her head. "It can wait. Can we go somewhere? Somewhere private?"

"Um, I haven't spoken to my sister yet, but she has enough distractions. I'm sure she won't miss me for a little longer."

They started walking toward the beach. All the while Elena searched for the right words. Was there such a thing? She hoped so.

"Elena? Hey, did you hear me?" Luca sent her a puzzled look.

"What did you say?"

"I said that you're really quiet today and you're starting to worry me."

He had no idea what was coming his way, and she felt bad for him. She didn't know whether to start with the tabloid story or the news of her pregnancy. Her stomach shivered with nerves.

Soon the worst will be over. It was the only positive thought she could dredge up, because her life was a scandalous mess.

CHAPTER EIGHT

WAS THERE ANY right way to say this?

Elena didn't think so. Maybe if they were a happy couple and madly in love. If that were the case, she'd do something cute—something memorable.

But in this case, she'd just have to settle for the blunt, honest truth.

They made their way down the long set of steps. She remained quiet, waiting until they were on the beach, where they wouldn't be disturbed. This conversation would be the most important one of her life. Once her feet touched the sand, she glanced up and down the beach, not spotting anyone.

"Okay. We're alone." Luca turned to face her. "What's bothering you?"

She gazed into his face. Her stomach started to churn again. And the words stuck in the back of her throat.

"Elena, you're really starting to worry me. Nothing can be this bad."

She nodded, trying to keep her emotions in check. "Yes, it can."

"Whatever it is, I'm here for you. You know that."

Her gaze rose to meet his. In his gaze, she found tenderness and warmth. She tried to impress that image upon her mind. She needed to remember this moment, because she doubted she'd see it again.

Where did she start? Did she blurt out about the pregnancy? Or did she start with the headlines? It was all such a mess.

She slipped off her shoes and started walking closer to the water. Letting the water wash over her feet always relaxed her in the past. She hoped it would do so again.

Luca walked beside her. He was quiet, as though giving her a moment to gather her thoughts. He was such a great guy. If he ever let down his guard, he'd make some woman a fantastic husband. It just wouldn't be her. They'd given it a shot in Paris, and it hadn't worked out. In fact, in the rays of the rising sun, it had gone from amazing to an utter disaster. The light of day had cast away all her silly romantic illusions and shed light on the stark reality—they did not belong together.

So what was she waiting for? It wasn't like they were a couple or even had a chance at a happily-ever-after. She might as well put it all out there and let the pieces fall as they may.

She stopped and turned to him. "This morning my mother found an article about me in the tabloids."

"And…"

She just couldn't look him in the eyes when she admitted the next part. She didn't want to see the disgust in his eyes. "And it had a picture of some loser kissing me. One of the headlines read, From Model to Home Wrecker!"

There was a slight pause as though he was digesting this news. "This is the guy you told me about in Paris?"

She nodded. "It's not true." She glanced up, willing him to believe her. "The whole thing is a twist of facts and lots of innuendo."

"I thought you ended things with him. That's what you said when I was in Paris."

"I did."

"Then how did they get a picture of you two kissing? And why is it showing up in the paper now?" Just as she predicted, his eyes were getting darker by the moment and clouds of doubt were forming.

Why did everyone in her life go for the worst-case scenario? Of course, the photo didn't help things. Before she could mount a reasonable defense, Luca pulled out his cell phone. And thanks to the beach being part of the royal grounds, the cell reception was excellent.

She wanted to beg him not to pull up the tabloid photo and article, but her pride resisted the urge. So what if he looked? It wouldn't change things. The tabloid was wrong. Surely he would see that. He knew her better. Knew that she would never knowingly cause problems in someone else's marriage.

She turned to stare out at the water. Usually she found it relaxing, but not today. Today all she could think about were all the mistakes she'd made in her life. And they seemed to be escalating this year. But that was going to stop. Here. And now. She had a baby to think about. She would do well by it.

She turned back to Luca. "There's more—"

"Did you read this?" His stormy gaze flickered to her and then back to the phone in his hand.

"It's nothing but lies."

"At the end, it says this jerk's wife filed for divorce. She's probably using this story as the basis for her multimillion-dollar settlement."

"And?"

He slipped his phone back in his pocket and stared at her. "Did you see this guy after you and I, well, after I visited you in Paris?"

"No. Of course not. Steven fooled me once with his flattery and lies. There's no way I would fall for his words again. I…I haven't seen anyone since you."

"And this story is the reason the press is at the palace gates?"

She lowered her head. "I had no idea they'd track me down here. I should leave Mirraccino."

"I can't think of any place better for you to be at this moment."

Her head lifted. "Really?"

"Yes. Here you have the best protection. No one will get near you. And eventually the paparazzi will get bored."

"I just don't understand why this is suddenly a story. I haven't seen Steven in almost three months."

His eyes momentarily widened, but then in a blink, his expression was unreadable. "Then I would say that picture suddenly appeared because the wife planted it, just in time for her to file for divorce."

"But the story made it sound like it just happened—as in yesterday."

"See, that's the thing. You were right here with me."

"Wait." She peered deep into his eyes. "You believe me?"

"Believe you? Of course I do. Why wouldn't I?"

She shrugged. "I don't know. I guess I'm just a bit on edge."

"Is this part of the reason you're in Mirraccino instead of in Paris, Milan or New York?"

She shook her head. "It has nothing to do with that story. In fact, there wasn't even a story until today."

"Then quit frowning. Everything will be all right. Give it one or two news cycles and the paparazzi will be on to another bit of sensationalized gossip." He reached out and pulled her into his arms.

She knew she should resist. She knew that things were complicated between them. But in that moment, she longed for the warmth and comfort she always felt in his arms. And so she let her body follow the pull of his arms.

Her chest pressed to his. Her arms wrapped around his trim waist. And her head landed on his broad shoulder. The stress ebbed away.

But then something happened that she hadn't been expecting. She breathed in his masculine scent, mingled with a spicy cologne. He smelled so good. She breathed in a little deeper. Oh, yes, she remembered being here—being held securely in his arms.

And it wasn't that long ago that they'd clung to each other like there was no tomorrow. Did he remember? Was that what he was thinking about right now?

Her whole body was alive with desire. It'd be so easy to turn her head just slightly and press her lips to the smooth skin of his neck. And then, realizing what she was about to do, she pulled away.

Luca gave her a puzzled look, and then he sighed. "Are you going to keep acting like this? Can't we just forget about what happened in Paris?"

She shook her head. "I can never forget."

"Sure you can, if you try. After all, we were friends a lot longer than we were lovers."

"Luca, quit trying to diminish it." That night had been very special to her even if it meant nothing to him.

He raked his fingers through his hair. "What can I do to make this better?"

"Nothing. Nothing at all."

"So that's it, we're always going to be awkward around each other? I can never put my arms around you to comfort you?"

"You don't understand. This isn't how I want things to be, but it's how they are."

"I don't understand. You're talking in circles."

He was right. She was being evasive on purpose. She was afraid to tell him that they would forever be linked.

"I'm pregnant." She hadn't intended to blurt it out, but at least it was finally out there.

"Pregnant?" Luca stumbled back a step as though the words had hit him with a one-two punch.

She nodded. The backs of her eyes stung with threatening tears. Darn hormones. She blinked repeatedly, refusing to play the emotional-woman card. She could get through the rest of this semirationally—she hoped.

His gaze searched hers. "You're sure?"

"Yes. I just saw the doctor last week for confirmation."

"Does he know? The guy in the photo?"

"Why would Steven know?"

"I would assume you'd tell the father, even if he's a total loser."

"I thought you believed me when I said it was only a kiss."

He shrugged. "People make mistakes. I thought maybe you were too embarrassed to admit it."

"First of all, he's not the father. Second, the baby's father is far from a loser. And lastly, I am telling him. Right now."

Luca's eyes momentarily widened. His lips pressed together into a firm line as the color drained from his face.

She'd never witnessed him speechless. He always had a quick comeback or a thoughtful comment. There was always something…until now.

The longer the silence dragged on, the more nervous she became. She had to do something, but what?

She knew this announcement was the last thing he'd expected to hear from her. "This was as much of a surprise for me as it is for you."

He shook his head as though he couldn't process it. He turned away and started walking—walking away from her. Just like he'd done in Paris. She'd let him go that time, but more than her broken heart was on the line this time.

She took off after him. "Luca, I know this is a shock. But we have to talk."

He stopped and faced her. The shocked look on his face told her just how caught off guard he was by this information. "Talk? Don't you think I deserve some time to absorb this information? After all, you've had how long?"

"A week or so. And I'm sorry I'm pushing this, but once the paparazzi finds out I'm pregnant, it's going to be a mess."

"Which won't be long, considering they're camping outside the palace gates." Luca turned and started walking again.

She walked with him. She hated having to push him, but the press was so close now. They were breathing down her neck—waiting for the next big headline. It was imperative that she and Luca do whatever they could to protect their child from scandal.

There was still so much to decide where the child was concerned. Would her child grow up here in Mirraccino? Doubtful. The only reason her parents lived on these amazing and sprawling grounds was because of her father's special affiliation with the king. If she wanted to move back to Mirraccino, she'd end up with an apartment in the city. Bellacitta was a thriving city that was a mix of old traditions and new technology. It certainly would be an interesting atmosphere to raise a child.

But she couldn't give up her future in Paris. If she remained there, her son or daughter would have the privilege of growing up in a city full of history, culture and endless ways to expand a young imagination. Luca could visit, or when she had time off, she could take their child to him. It would work out somehow.

But Luca wasn't helping her find any of those answers. She needed him to say something, or at least acknowledge what she'd told him.

She reached out, grabbing his arm. "Please, Luca, talk to me."

He stopped and faced her. "What do you want from me?"

"I don't know. I guess just to talk to me. Maybe to say that everything will be okay."

"Okay?" He ran his hand over the top of his hair, scattering the short, dark spikes. And then he expelled an audible sigh. "Just tell me one thing. Is it really my baby?"

Ouch! His question dug straight into her heart. Not so long ago, they'd accepted each other's words as fact without having to question. Obviously things had changed more than she'd ever imagined.

"I swear on my life that this baby is yours and mine. I didn't come to you expecting anything. I have enough of my own money to take care of the two of us. I just wanted you to know. It was the right thing to do."

"Then I would say, no, things aren't going to be all right. Those reporters at the palace gate, they are waiting for you and it has nothing to do with your work."

Elena's gaze lowered, and she shook her head. "They'll want some comment about the photo. But I didn't do anything they said. I went on a few dates with Steven. That's it. He told me he was divorced and lonely."

"How could you not know who he is?"

"He gave me a fictitious name, and quite frankly, I don't read the finance section of the paper. And he didn't give me any reason to doubt him." She worried her bottom lip as she internally berated herself. "I was such a fool."

"But smart enough not to sleep with him."

"Thank goodness."

There was one real reason why that wasn't an option for her. Steven didn't stack up to Luca. And though she tried not to, she couldn't help but compare everyone to Luca. Did that make her pathetic? She hoped not.

"And what will happen when they find out you're pregnant?" Luca looked worried. "The paparazzi is going to jump to conclusions, just like they did with that photo. They are going to tell the world that jerk is the father of my baby!"

There was so much emotion in that statement that Elena was caught off guard. Perhaps she'd been telling herself that he wouldn't care about the baby because he didn't care about her romantically—to soften his rejection. So where exactly did that leave them besides in a mess?

CHAPTER NINE

A BABY.

My baby.

Luca was having problems processing it all. A rush of emotions hit him like a tsunami. They swept away his breath and left him feeling unsteady.

I'm going to be a father.

Those were words he never thought he'd say. A tiny human was counting on him to get this right. Luca's gaze moved to Elena's still-flat midsection. It was so hard to believe there was a little human growing in there.

Luca raked a shaky hand through his hair. "Wow! This is a lot to take in."

"I know it is. Maybe I should go so you can think. Just know that I don't expect anything of you." She started to turn away.

"Wait. What?" Surely he hadn't heard her correctly.

"This mess with Steven, it's not your problem. I'll figure something out."

"Like what?"

She shrugged. "Maybe I'll just let the press have their say and ignore them. Eventually they'll catch on to a new story—a bigger story."

Luca shook his head. "No way. I refuse to let that scum be linked to our child."

"Like you can stop that from happening."

This was his moment to step up—to do the right thing. He'd never had anyone count on him so completely. The responsibility was enormous. He had no idea how to be a parent.

But he did know that no other man was going to take credit for fathering his child. No way! He refused to let that happen. He needed to head off the ensuing scandal. And there was only one way he could think of.

"We'll get married."

Elena shook her head in confusion. "I don't think I heard you correctly."

"Yes, you did. You and I, we're getting married."

"No."

"Yes. We have to. It's the only way."

Her eyes narrowed. "Did you just demand that I marry you?"

Had he? He supposed it might have sounded that way. Surely she had to see the logic of such a move. "This is what's best."

She shook her head. "No way. It's not what's best for me."

"Then think of our baby."

"I am thinking of the baby. And you forcing me into a loveless marriage isn't going to make any of us happy. Don't you remember Paris? That night—well, it didn't work out. Why in the world would you want to compound that mistake?"

"Because as you pointed out, this is about a lot more than you and me. There's the baby to consider. He or she will be the DiSalvo heir."

"Oh." The dejected look on her face told him that he'd said something wrong, but for the life of him he didn't know what it was.

"What does 'oh' mean?"

"Nothing. I'm just surprised."

"That I would want to marry you in order to protect our child?"

"I'm surprised that you would propose marriage at all. I thought you were a proclaimed bachelor."

"I was." He still wasn't comfortable with the idea of making a commitment. He hadn't had time to let it all settle in his mind. But time was running out before the press added two and two and got five. "Come on. Let's go."

"Go where?"

He sighed. Why wasn't she following this? "To get married. Once we do that, the problem is solved and the paparazzi will back off."

"Maybe it will fix one problem, but what about all the other problems it will create?" She shook her head. "I can't. I won't. I know you well enough to know that you don't want to get married, much less have children. I shouldn't have told you—"

"Yes, you should have. I don't know why you're fighting me on this. You have to see that I'm right."

"I don't see that. Just let me take care of this. You won't have to be bothered with me…or the baby. I'll go back to Paris and I'll refuse to name the father."

Was she even listening to what he was saying? She was going to compound this problem, whereas he planned to head it off from the start. "You'll just add fuel to the fire. The gossip will grow with every news cycle. By not naming me, it'll be like confirming that jerk is indeed the father."

She frowned. "Maybe you're right, but I can't do it. Binding us both to a…to a fake marriage, it just won't work."

He had to admit that she deserved better than to marry someone who couldn't love her the way she deserved to be loved. Perhaps he was broken inside. He hadn't chosen to shut down after his mother's death. It had just happened to him, like a raging case of the flu. No one wants it. No one expects it. And then pow! It hits you.

At least with the flu, you recover. Whatever happened to him the day his mother died, it hadn't gone away. His feelings just shut down—much like his father.

And so marriage had never been on his wish list. He knew it could become emotional warfare. All that emotional baggage wasn't something he wanted in his life.

But this was about so much more than what Elena deserved and what he wanted—there was now a baby involved. And this was no ordinary baby—it was the DiSalvo heir. His secret heir.

He cleared his throat. "Marriage is the only way I can think of to protect our child and give him or her a legitimate claim to their heritage."

Elena didn't move for a moment. And when she spoke, it was so soft that he had to strain to hear her. "Perhaps you're right." She paused as though gathering her thoughts. "On some level, your idea makes some sense—"

"Good. We have to do what is right for the child." He was finally getting through to her. He drew in a deep breath, hoping that everything was finally resolved. "Elena, I'm going to ask you one more time. Will you agree to marry me?"

"No." There wasn't even the slightest hesitation in her quick answer. She waved her hands, as though to chase away the idea. "I…I can't do this." A tear slipped down her cheek, and she swiped it away. "It's too much. Too fast. Too…wrong."

"Elena, don't do this. Don't do this to us—to our child."

This time it was Elena who took off down the beach, but she wasn't walking. She was running. Her long hair fluttered in the breeze.

Luca swore as he watched her run away from him. He'd never imagined if he proposed to someone she would run away in tears. Why did it seem as though he was always making Elena cry?

Part of him wanted to let her keep running until she wore herself out. And the other part of him wanted to go to her and comfort her. He was torn by the tumultuous emotions. And for a man used to keeping his emotions in check, this was a lot.

He realized that from this day forward, he would have

not one but two people to worry about—to protect. He knew just how unpredictable life could be, and he couldn't imagine living through another loss. His heart just couldn't take it.

And it didn't help that Elena was already a darling of the paparazzi. Her life was routinely on display for all the world to see—including potential stalkers.

However, his father would be thrilled to know the DiSalvo line would continue—someone to carry on the lemon grove. If there was still something to hand down. And that was Luca's fault. He shouldn't have let the distance between them become a yawning canyon with no footbridge to connect them.

But that problem was going to have to wait. First, he had to convince Elena to marry him. Knowing her as well as he did, she wouldn't make it easy on him.

And so he had to make it hard for her to turn him down.

He reached for his phone. This was going to take some work, but he would make her his bride in short order. And he would claim his baby—his baby. The words sounded surreal.

Life certainly did change on the spin of a coin.

Yesterday, he'd had a firm grip on his life. And today, he and Elena were having a baby.

And somehow, some way, they were getting married.

He'd make it happen. But it was going to take a little more forethought than he'd first envisioned. And he had no time to waste.

CHAPTER TEN

SHE WAS TRAPPED.

The paparazzi was camped out on the perimeter of the palace gates like leeches, just waiting to suck the life out of her.

Elena turned away from the roving cameras of the press. She'd been hoping that their fascination with her would end quickly, but that wasn't to be. It was open season on her life, and the reporter with the first exposé or telling photo would make a bundle.

And after speaking with Lauren Renard, Elena learned the painful truth—she'd been dropped from the fashion line. All her scheduled shoots had been canceled. Her contract was to be voided. And her name was on the lips of everyone in the know throughout Paris.

Without being spotted, Elena retreated to the royal gardens. Where she normally took solace in the serenity of the colorful blossoms and the gentle, perfumed air, today she didn't notice any of it. Her insides were tied up in knots. What was she going to do?

Luca's parting words kept repeating in her mind like a broken record.

Don't do this to us—to our child.

Normally, she'd blow off such a rushed, heat-of-the-moment proposal. No one would mean such a thing. After all, it wasn't like they were a couple. This pregnancy, it wasn't supposed to happen. *They* weren't meant to happen.

But a marriage proposal from Luca was different. He was not a man to throw around such words whether casually or in the heat of the moment. She knew him—or at least she thought she did. But everything had changed so dramatically between them since that night in Paris. Now, she questioned whether she'd ever known him at all.

Too restless to sit down, she started walking with no destination in mind. She moved past the garden gates and into the field of sunflowers. Blind to the world around her, she could only envision the *what if*s and *might have*s that this pregnancy had brought into her world.

She moved to the cliff overlooking the sand and sea. The breeze rushed past her, combing through her hair. Despite the beauty of this particular spot with the azure-blue sky, the sunshine dancing upon the water and the sailboat in the distance bobbing with each swell, all Elena could think about was that her life had come to a fork in the road.

The decisions she was about to make were so much more enormous than when she'd had to choose between attending college here on the island or pursuing a modeling career in Paris. To a young girl of eighteen who had led a sheltered life, venturing to a big city—even one as romantic as Paris—had still been a scary idea, especially when she knew absolutely no one there.

But now she had to make a decision not only for herself, but also for her child. The road to the left was one for just her and her baby. It would be them against the world. And if she took the road to the right, she envisioned herself holding her child's hand with Luca holding their child's other hand. Which was the right answer for all of them?

She started to walk again. Her head pulsed with chaotic thoughts of possible scenarios for her future. Her hand pressed to her midsection, feeling a protective instinct that she'd never felt before. She might disagree with Luca on numerous things, but there was one thing they agreed on. They had to do what was right for their child.

Their child.

The words stuck in her mind. As much as she wanted to make all the decisions about this baby, she couldn't.

They'd created this tiny life together, and it was only right that they share the decisions. It was her first solid resolution, and it felt right.

And then another thought came to her: she downright refused to be dictated to by Luca or anyone else. In that moment, it didn't matter to her one iota that Luca was an earl or that his uncle was the king. They would make decisions together—she would not bend to his will.

Elena stopped walking. Suddenly she was feeling a bit better. Her jumbled thoughts were starting to gain some clarity. Even the pounding in her head was starting to subside.

When she glanced around, she realized that she'd been drawn back to one of her childhood haunts. And it was looking none too good. The little cabin had been abandoned eons ago, but as kids, she and Luca had worked to patch up the roof with branches and leaves. They made it into their secret clubhouse.

She stepped inside and glanced up, finding most of the roof was now gone. So much for their repairs. She smiled at the memory of them working so hard together. Back then, it was so much easier for them to communicate.

Why couldn't life be like it used to be?

The sound of an engine cut through her thoughts. It was getting closer. Who in the world would be riding around out here at the far reaches of the royal estate? And then she realized that it was probably the security guards making their rounds.

She stepped outside to let them know of her presence, not wanting to alarm them. But when her gaze adjusted to the bright sunshine, she found that it was not a guard seated behind the wheel of the navy blue Jeep with the royal crest emblazoned across the hood. It was Luca.

He jumped out. "So this is where you ended up?"

"I...uh, was just walking."

"That's some walk. It's been a few hours since you left me on the beach."

"I had a lot of thinking to do." She wasn't so sure she wanted to get into it all now. "How did you find me?"

"After I checked your parents' place and the gardens, this place came to mind. You always used to come here when you were upset." He stepped past her and entered the cabin. He looked around before returning to her side. "I wonder if our child will find this spot and make it their clubhouse."

"I…I don't know." She supposed that it was a possibility when she visited her parents.

Luca moved to stand in front of her. "Listen, I'm sorry about earlier. I didn't handle that very well."

"You're right. You didn't." And surprisingly, she wasn't furious with him any longer. "How about we write it off to shock? You didn't know what you were saying."

"But see, that wouldn't be the truth." He reached out for her hand, but she stepped back. "I did mean it when I said we should get married."

She shook her head. "Not like this. I don't want anyone to marry me because they have to."

"It's not that way." He shifted his weight. "I could walk away, but I'm not."

Elena let out a nervous laugh. "I can hear it now. At one of your sister's parties, someone will ask, 'And how did Luca propose to you?' And I'll say, 'He fell on his sword to save me and my child from the monstrous press.'" She shook her head, dispelling the awful scene. "Not exactly the romantic beginning to a marriage that a girl would hope for."

His eyes widened as though a thought had just come to him.

She didn't want to know his new idea. It was best that they end things here while they were still speaking to one another.

She lifted her chin and met his gaze. "I should be going."

"Wait." He reached for her hand. "I know I messed things up when I proposed to you earlier—"

"You didn't propose." Her gaze narrowed. "You practically ordered me to marry you."

His mouth opened, but nothing came out. And then at least he had the decency to look a tad embarrassed.

As much as she'd like to tell him that his idea of them getting married was preposterous, she couldn't. She hadn't thought of any other way to protect the baby and pass on the proper legacy their child deserved. If she were to marry Luca, their child would fit in—unlike her, who was forever on the outside looking in.

Luca craned his neck, looking at their surroundings. What was he looking for?

"Of all the places with flowers on this estate, why couldn't there be some here?" he said with a sigh.

"Flowers?" It took her a moment to realize that he wanted to collect them for her. Her heart picked up its pace at the realization that he was trying to do this proposal thing properly. "I don't need flowers. But I do need us to come to terms."

"Terms? What sort of terms?"

"I agree with you. Our child deserves to have their legacy. But this will be a marriage on paper only."

"Are you sure that's what you want?"

Was he hoping that she'd change her mind? She couldn't quite tell by his tone. Or was he making sure she didn't want more from him than he was willing to offer?

"I'm sure. We'll have separate beds and separate lives."

"Not so fast on the separate lives. If we want everyone, including the paparazzi, to believe the baby is mine, we're going to have to present a happy front."

He was right. Still, she hesitated. Could she really agree to this arrangement? It was so cold and calculated.

Luca took a steadying breath and then dropped to his knee. He took her hand in his. And then he gazed up into her eyes.

"Luca, what are you doing?"

"Proposing. If you'll let me."

"But you don't have to—"

"I want to."

"And what about your sister?"

He frowned. "What does any of this have to do with Annabelle?"

"It's her week. You know, *her* engagement celebration."

"And?"

"And we can't let anyone know that we've gotten engaged. It'll overshadow Annabelle's moment in the spotlight."

"First of all, I'm not proposing an engagement. I want you to elope with me. Today. Right now. As for my sister..." Luca rubbed the back of his neck. "We won't tell anyone about our marriage until after the reception on Saturday. Okay?"

Elena's heart was pounding so hard that it echoed in her ears. "But—"

"Shush. Let me do this before I forget what I'm going to say."

She pressed a hand to her mouth, but her gaze never left his. This was it. He was going to propose and then they were to be married. It would all be done so quickly, so neatly. No fanfare. No frilly dress. No romantic moments.

And yet, she could not deny that it was best for their child. She could no longer put her needs and wants first. She was about to be a mother.

"Elena, we've known each other since we were little kids playing in the palace gardens. You've been there with me through the best and worst times of my life. Somehow it seems fitting that we are pledging to join our lives officially. I promise to always be there for you and for our child. Will you marry me?"

Tears ran down her cheeks. Instead of tears of joy, they were tears of sadness. This wasn't how she'd imagined this moment working out. And her pregnancy hormones were working overtime, making her a sappy mess.

He removed the ring from his pinkie. "I know you're expecting a diamond, but I didn't have a chance to get you one. I hope you don't mind if I use this as a temporary substitute under the circumstances."

She gazed down at the gold ring with his family's crest engraved upon it. Luca held it poised at the end of her finger. She couldn't believe that this was all really happening. It was like she was moving through a dream.

And then she nodded her head. "Yes, I'll marry you— we'll marry you."

He placed one hand over her still-flat abdomen. With the other hand, he slid the ring on her finger. It was a little tight, but it would do.

This was the beginning of a whole new future for her, him and their baby.

CHAPTER ELEVEN

THE HEAVILY TINTED town car eased out of the palace gates.

It appeared the paparazzi was off chasing another story.

Elena breathed a sigh of relief.

But that was just the first hurdle. They still had to conduct a secret wedding. Just the thought of exchanging *I do*s with Luca made her stomach quiver. When she was a teenager, she'd imagined that one day they might marry. But that was when she was still young and foolish. After all, he was an earl, one day to become a duke, and at the time she'd been a nobody. Why would he have ever considered marrying her?

It wasn't until much later in life that she realized all of Luca's grumbling and resentment about the institution of marriage wasn't just a smoke screen to keep her at bay. He really meant it. She'd felt sorry for him. She couldn't imagine living such a lonely life and never allowing anyone to get close.

And now she was dooming herself to a loveless marriage. She banished the thought as soon as it came to her. There was no backing out now. Luca had made a flurry of phone calls. The arrangements were in motion.

Elena pressed a hand to her abdomen, thinking about their unborn child. At least their son or daughter would now be legitimate. They wouldn't be excluded and press their nose to the glass to see all the dressed-up people at the formal dinners and balls. That thought was what kept her quiet as the black town car ushered them through the streets of Bellacitta.

They'd already stopped at the jewelry store, the courthouse and the dress shop, and now they were headed to a little chapel just outside the city—a place where they would have the privacy to say their vows without the paparazzi lurking about.

She nervously played with Luca's ring that was still on her ring finger. She remembered when he'd received the ring from his father. He'd been thirteen. His father had told him that he was growing into a man and this was his future—his destiny.

She had been awed not only by the beautiful ring with the intricate crest, but also the fact that Luca had a destiny to fulfill. She didn't have any such thing. Her family was ordinary, and she'd always longed to be extraordinary. And she'd almost done it. She had been on her way to having one of the most famous faces in the world.

But now she was pregnant. Her future as a model was over. Sure, she could lose the weight. Maybe she could avoid stretch marks. But even if she could regain the same figure—and that was a big *if*—she would have lost her traction in the business. Her slot would be filled by younger, more glamorous girls. She would forever be playing catch-up, and in the process, her child would only get bits and pieces of her time.

"What has you so quiet?" Luca asked as he leaned back against the black leather upholstery.

"Just thinking how far we've come since you received this ring from your father."

"It seems like a lifetime ago."

"Will your father be happy about the baby?" She hoped so. She wanted her child to be surrounded by love.

"My father will be over the moon that I'm finally doing what he's always wanted—settling down with a family and taking over the business."

"Wait." She sat up straight and turned to him. "You're taking over the business? Since when? What about your job in Milan?"

"Things have changed since I've been here. Certain matters have come to light, but we don't need to get into all that now. We have a wedding to go to."

"You're sure you want to go through with this marriage?" Elena asked for about the fifth time that afternoon.

"Quit asking. The answer is always going to be the same. Yes, I want to marry you."

If only he meant that for all the right reasons. She had no illusions about this marriage lasting, and so she would have to guard her heart. Letting herself think this marriage was anything but a show would be a disaster for her and her child. She had to stay strong for her unborn baby.

He'd never imagined that he'd be doing this.

Luca stood at the front of the chapel in his new suit. While Elena had picked out a white dress for the ceremony, he'd decided that a new suit was in order. Luckily, they had one in his size.

He resisted the urge to tug at his collar as the pianist played the wedding march. This was it. He was doing the one thing he'd vowed never to do—getting married.

But if he had to marry anyone, he was thankful it was Elena. They were compatible. Or at least they used to be. They'd shared more than twenty years of friendship. Surely they could draw on that and find common ground.

And then she appeared at the end of the aisle. It didn't matter that there were no guests. They had asked the photographer and his assistant to bear witness, and that was all they needed. The only important people were standing right here in this historic chapel.

As she made her way up the aisle, the photographer took numerous pictures. Elena seemed surprised that there was a photographer present, but with the help of Luca's assistant, he'd tended to as many wedding details that he could think of. And he figured that with the lack of any family present, Elena could share these photos with family and friends.

But he wouldn't need any photos.

There was no way he would forget his beautiful bride. Her dress was white and tea length, falling just below her knees. The straps were off the shoulder and the bodice fit her snugly. It was as if the dress had been made for her. She took his breath away. Too bad this wasn't a real marriage— wait, had he really thought that?

Before he could delve further into his thoughts, Elena stepped up to his side. With one hand clasping a colorful bouquet of pink and white peonies, she slipped her free hand into his.

The older minister peered at them over his reading glasses. "Have you both come here of your own free will?"

Luca felt the initial tightening of Elena's hand. He willed her to stay calm. He knew she didn't want to marry him but that she would do it for the love of their child.

"I have," Elena said softly.

"I have, too."

And so the minister went through the ceremony. Luca didn't know what he expected to feel, but as the minister said, "Until death do us part," Luca felt the walls go up around him. He knew he shouldn't shut down, but he couldn't help it. The devastation of his mother's murder still had lingering effects.

He'd witnessed how his father had utterly withdrawn from their family after his mother died. His father had always been working and never had time for his children— children who were hurting, too, and left to find their way through the darkness alone.

Luca couldn't imagine giving his heart to Elena—if she even wanted it—and then losing her. It was better to keep a wall between them. It was safer. For both of them.

But above all, this marriage would allow Luca to claim his heir—the future of the DiSalvo name. Luca's father would have no choice but to recognize that Luca was now all grown up and responsible—responsible enough to take over the family business and turn it around. Where he'd once felt a family obligation to fix things when his father asked for help, Luca now felt driven to keep the business and the title viable. It was a new experience for him.

"I now pronounce you husband and wife. You may kiss the bride."

Elena looked at him with a wide-eyed stare. It wasn't exactly the passionate look that he'd expected to find on his bride's face. Still, it was up to them to convince people that the marriage was real—no matter how temporary.

His gaze dipped to her pink, glossy lips. Her mouth had tormented him each night in his dreams. Her sweet kisses had left him longing for more. And now he had the perfect excuse to kiss her once more.

But he hesitated. Common sense told him to make it a quick peck. He could feel the minister's expectant gaze on him.

Luca pulled Elena close. And for a moment, he stared into her eyes. They were the most beautiful shade of forget-me-nots. The name was most fitting, as her eyes were quite memorable. In fact, they were totally unforgettable. Every time he stared into her eyes, it was like she spun a spell over him. Just like now…

His head lowered and he claimed her lips. And then, forgetting about this being a quick peck, he drew her even closer. In that moment, nothing mattered but them. Forgetting that they were still in the church, he deepened the kiss. Elena opened her mouth, welcoming him inside. Her kiss was extraordinary, and he didn't think he would ever take it, or her, for granted.

He didn't want to let her go. Because once he released her, he knew that the wall dividing them would immediately come back up. And though it might be safe behind that wall, it was also cold and lonely. But with Elena in his arms, there was a warmth growing and spreading within his chest.

Just then Elena pressed her palms to his chest and pulled back from him. Reality came crashing back in, popping the bubble of happiness that had momentarily encapsulated them. Luca glanced away, not wanting her to realize how that kiss had moved him.

Luca realized that going forward he had to be careful around her. Happiness didn't last. He'd learned that lesson the hard way. First, with his mother dying. And finally with his father hiding within his work and ignoring his children.

Luca had done the only thing he knew how to do at the time—let loose and lived life to its fullest—even risking life and limb routinely. But now he knew how to curb those urges. He knew how to tuck his feelings into that little box in his chest.

He could do this—he could be the public husband Elena needed. And he could be the father to his child that his father had never been to him.

CHAPTER TWELVE

So now what?

Elena sat next to Luca as their chauffeured car made its way across the city. She stared at her bridal bouquet. She was now Mrs. DiSalvo.

With the shock of what they'd just done starting to wear off, reality was hitting her hard. A whole gamut of emotions warred within her, leaving her stomach in a knot.

Elena DiSalvo. Mrs. DiSalvo. Mrs. Luca DiSalvo.

And what was up with that kiss at the altar? If that had all been for show, it was quite convincing—too convincing. There was more to that kiss than Luca doing his husbandly duty. If he was hoping to change her mind about sharing a bed, it wasn't going to happen. No matter how many heart-fluttering kisses he plied on her.

She glanced over at Luca, but he appeared preoccupied with his phone. She wondered if this was what their future would be like if they were to stay together—awkward and quiet. The funny thing was, before they'd slept together, their relationship had flowed easily. Before that night, they'd been able to laugh and joke around. But now, post-sex, things were so different.

She gazed out the window at the passing cityscape. This definitely wasn't the way back to the palace. "Luca, where are we going?"

"You'll find out soon enough."

"But your sister will be wondering where we went."

"I'm certain my sister is well distracted by her new fiancé."

Elena couldn't argue with that statement. Annabelle had never looked happier than she had this week. She was practically glowing.

That was the way a woman should look when she was getting married. It wasn't how Elena had looked today. And she knew it was selfish, because they'd done what they needed to for their baby. But she couldn't help but feel as though she'd missed out on something very profound and moving.

Sadness crept over Elena. This wasn't how she'd envisioned her wedding day. When she was younger, she'd dreamed about her wedding being the happiest day of her life. Of rose petals lining her path, with her family looking on and her eager groom awaiting her at the end of the aisle.

She stared blindly out the window. Tears pricked the backs of her eyes, but she blinked repeatedly, willing them away. After all, those had been dreams of a gullible young girl. She was now a mature woman who knew that life rarely lived up to anyone's dreams.

This marriage was a means to an end. A business arrangement of sorts. Try as she might, none of those explanations soothed the throb in her chest.

The car slowed down and turned into an underground garage. Elena was jarred from her thoughts, but it was too late to look around to figure out where they were. She was certainly confused.

"Luca, what have you done?"

His brows scrunched together. "Why do you make it sound like I've done something wrong?"

"I don't know. Have you?"

"Certainly not. I just thought the occasion deserved something extra."

"Extra?" She had no idea what he meant by that comment.

And Luca wasn't offering any other clues.

When the car pulled to a stop, the driver opened the door for her. She stepped out into the garage next to a bank of elevators. Luca rounded the car and took her hand. He led her to the farthest elevator and pressed a button. Instantly the doors swept open. Inside he swiped a card and pressed another button labeled PH1.

"Luca, what are you up to?"

"It's a surprise."

"Don't you think we've had enough of those for one day?" The excitement of the day really had taken a lot out of her. Especially as she found herself getting tired easier than normal since she'd become pregnant.

"I promise, soon you can rest."

She sent him an I-don't-believe-you look. "Just tell me what you're up to."

He didn't say a word as he stared straight ahead.

The anticipation was getting to her. She had to admit that normally she loved surprises and Luca knew it. But today was far from normal. What in the world did he have planned?

The doors swished open to reveal an expansive suite decorated mostly in white with strategically placed wine-colored accents. One wall consisted of floor-to-ceiling windows that looked out over the beautiful city. The soft golden rays from the setting sun gave the place a warm, inviting glow.

She turned to Luca. "I don't understand."

And then, without warning, Luca lifted her into his arms.

"What are you doing? Put me down."

"Smile for the camera." Luca smiled and nodded toward the photographer and his assistant, who had been at the church.

She forced a smile while the photographer snapped one photo after the next.

"Could I have one of you two kissing before you put her down?" the photographer asked. He obviously wasn't in on the fact that their marriage was for show only.

"Of course," Luca said a little too eagerly. And then he looked at her as though begging her to just go with it.

Luca's hands gripped her tighter as he rolled her body closer to his. As his face drew closer, her pulse raced. This wasn't a good idea. And yet neither moved to stop it.

Their gazes met and held. In the background, the camera flashed. But for Elena, all she could see was the desire reflected in Luca's eyes. Was she looking at him the same way?

He didn't have to beg. The truth was that she enjoyed his kisses, a lot. A whole lot.

Just then he pressed his lips to hers. Was it wrong that she was grateful for this excuse to kiss him? And what would happen when their excuses for being intimate faded away?

She'd be left with these delicious memories. And so she took advantage of the moment. She wrapped her arms around his neck and deepened the kiss. He tasted minty and delicious. And his kiss was filled with passion and promises of more.

Elena couldn't write off the rush of desire as a little too much champagne, because she hadn't had any. Nor would she have any in her condition. So did that mean all these rising emotions were real?

Luca pulled back and gently lowered her feet to the ground. His gaze met hers. They stared at each other for a moment as though they were each trying to figure out what had just happened. But with the photographer walking them through various poses—from sipping nonalcoholic apple cider to cutting the cake—they didn't get a chance to discuss what had happened during that kiss. Maybe it was for the best. Emotions were running high today, and it was hard to tell what was real and what was an exaggeration.

And then there was their first dance as husband and wife. Luca knew she enjoyed jazz, and so he put on "It

Had to Be You" by Tony Bennett and Carrie Underwood. The volume was just right to wrap around them, cocooning them from the outside world and transporting them to a place where normal rules didn't apply.

She paused for a second, wondering if Luca had picked out this specific song on purpose. It wouldn't be unrealistic. She hadn't missed his detailed level of planning for this rushed wedding. If she wasn't careful, she'd start to get caught up in this fantasy and believe that this wedding was real in every aspect.

The rays of the setting sun on the distant horizon painted the penthouse a warm gold. The piano music played and Tony Bennett's soft voice filled the air about them. This whole scenario was amazingly romantic.

As Luca's arms wrapped around her, her thoughts went back in time. When they were kids and weren't permitted to attend the palace balls, she would put on her finest dress and Luca would be in his school uniform. They would dance in the grand foyer. They'd both ended up laughing as they pretended to be all grown up and used proper mannerisms.

But tonight there was no pretending. They were adults, and being proper didn't appear to be on the agenda this evening. Luca held her close—quite close. And it was taking all of her will not to rest her cheek against his shoulder.

When her body accidentally brushed against Luca, need flared within her. She wanted her husband with every fiber of her body. Her insides heated up as desire pooled in her core.

The breath caught in her throat. *This can't be happening.* She couldn't give in to her longings.

Luca leaned close and whispered, "Relax."

The way his breath tickled her ear sent goose bumps racing down her arms. All the while, she had to think about something else—anything but the way her body was responding to Luca's. She focused on the lyrics of the song playing in the background. It was a duet, and they were singing about finding that special someone and how fate played a role.

But Elena hadn't found that special someone. She wasn't even looking. She didn't want to be lied to again.

Not that Luca would lie. He'd tell her straight up that he didn't love her. He had a double-reinforced wall about his heart and there was no breaking through it. He made sure of it.

The thought made her sad.

This wedding—this whole day—was too realistic. And yet, it was all a show. She couldn't let herself get caught up in it. Even the song was surely just a coincidence.

The backs of her eyes burned with unshed tears. These darn hormones had her reacting to things that she would otherwise be able to shrug off.

Luca continued to twirl her around the floor. She attempted to put a respectable distance between them. Because if she wasn't careful, she was going to get swept up in this piece of fiction. In the end, she would have nothing but a broken heart. And that would forever ruin her relationship with Luca. How could they raise a child together if nothing existed between them but hostility?

Just then the music switched to a love song by Frank Sinatra. The beautiful lyrics made her think of everything they were both deprived of by this empty marriage. They were doomed to live a lie.

Oh, no! This is just too much.

Elena pulled herself out of Luca's arms. Her gaze sought out the hallway and then she ran. She didn't know where she was running to, but she just couldn't pretend to be the loving bride any longer. The photo session was over. The whole thing was over. This was a mistake. A big mistake.

She just needed a few minutes to gather herself. And for

those stupid love songs to stop playing. She didn't want to think about how things were supposed to be. She was having enough problems dealing with how things were.

Elena ran to the first bedroom she came across and threw the door shut with a resounding thud. She willed Luca not to follow. She didn't know what to say to make this situation all right for both of them.

CHAPTER THIRTEEN

ONE MOMENT SHE was in his arms…

The next she was gone.

Luca stood there, watching as his wife ran away from him.

What had happened? He thought he was doing a good thing. He knew that Elena never imagined this for her wedding, but he'd wanted to give her some nice memories. He'd tried to remember all her favorite things, from the chocolate cake with raspberry ganache to the jazz music.

It hadn't been easy to arrange this evening on the spur of the moment, but thankfully he had a well-connected assistant. He had every intention of bribing her to follow him to Halencia. He could well imagine his perfect assistant handling the business while he was spending time with his family.

That was, if he still had a family. Why had Elena run off?

Maybe he'd tried too hard.

The thought was driven home by the lyrics of love reverberating off the walls and enveloping him. That had definitely been a miscalculation. What did they say? That hindsight was crystal clear? In that moment, he knew exactly what that meant.

Luca strode over to the stereo system and switched off the music. And then he turned to the photographer and his assistant. After thanking them for making room for them in their schedule, Luca showed them to the door. He didn't give them any explanations—mainly because he didn't have any.

He wished he knew exactly what had upset his bride.

Was it the music? Was she that miserable being married to him? Or was it the pregnancy hormones?

Was it wrong that he hoped for the last option?

Luca rubbed the back of his neck and stared down the hallway. It seemed like a lifetime since he'd been able to talk to Elena casually. Before Paris, he'd known how to make her smile. He'd known which words to say to encourage her when one of her projects seemed insurmountable. He'd known how to make her laugh out loud until happy tears pooled in her eyes.

And yet, he realized it really wasn't that long ago that he'd had his best friend. If only he hadn't broken the cardinal rule of best friends—don't sleep together. Since that unforgettable night, he'd lost his ability to speak to Elena without upsetting her. And this evening was no exception.

With much trepidation, he stopped in front of the closed bedroom door. He still didn't have a clue what to say to her. *I'm sorry*? But he wasn't sure what he was sorry for.

He rapped his knuckles on the door. "Elena?"

No answer.

"Elena, please talk to me."

Again, there was no answer. Worry settled in.

He knocked again. "Elena, I'm coming in."

He tried the doorknob, but it was locked. Surely she didn't feel that she had to lock the door around him. What in the world was happening to them?

"Elena, you're worrying me. Please tell me you're all right."

"I'm fine."

He breathed a sigh of relief. "Will you let me in so we can talk?"

"No. I don't want to talk."

Now what? He wasn't just going to walk away. There had to be a way to fix things. He lowered himself to the floor. He leaned his back against the doorjamb.

"I'm not going anywhere," he said as a matter of fact. "I'm going to stay right here until we work this out."

No response.

He would keep talking and hopefully he would get through to her. It'd worked in the past. But that had been when they were kids, when Elena hadn't understood why he got to do things at the royal palace that she was not permitted to do. At the time, he hadn't understood, either. When you're a kid, social status doesn't mean anything, especially when the person in question is your best friend. But now that their circumstances had shifted dramatically, he didn't know how to deal with the changing landscape.

If he was this confused, he couldn't imagine that Elena was doing any better, considering she was pregnant. The thought of the baby—his baby, *their* baby—was still mind-blowing. And maybe the wedding celebration on top of it all had been a bad choice.

He leaned his head against the door. "I only meant to make you happy today. I heard you on the beach when you said you wanted to be able to tell people about your engagement. I thought that would extend to your wedding. I wanted to make it a special memory for you. I knew I couldn't give you the magical day you've always dreamed of, but I tried to make it not so depressing."

This was so much harder than he'd ever imagined. "I know ours isn't a marriage made of love, but it's one based on a lifetime of friendship. Maybe it will be stronger than others. Because whether you believe it or not, I'm still your friend. I know that you hate peas. That you're afraid of horror movies. And that your favorite color is purple. And I really, really miss my friend. Is there any chance I can have her back?"

The silence dragged on, and he didn't know what else to say.

Then the lock clicked, and the door snicked open. And

there stood Elena. He got to his feet. The sadness in her eyes ripped at his heart. Was he responsible for all this?

He didn't think about it; he just reacted. He reached out and pulled her into his arms. And to his surprise, she wrapped her arms around him. Her head rested on his shoulder.

This right here—it was right. He felt calm and centered when she was in his arms. Or maybe it was because she wasn't upset with him any longer. It didn't matter. He just had to keep the peace. It was good for them and it was good for the baby.

When they pulled apart, he noticed the tear marks that had smudged her makeup. He didn't say a word about it and pretended he didn't notice. He took her by the hand, which he immediately noticed was cold.

He guided her over to the bed, where they sat side by side. She picked up something. It looked like a slip of paper. The way she held it made it seem important.

"What do you have there?" he asked.

Her gaze moved to him and then back to the paper. "It's a picture of our baby."

That was the last thing he'd expected her to say. The thought of seeing their baby for the first time filled him with anxiety. It would make this so real—so binding.

Suddenly he felt trapped, and the walls were closing in on him. He got to his feet and started to pace. This wasn't how an expectant father was supposed to feel. What was wrong with him? He'd failed his family, and now he was about to fail his child.

"Don't you even want to see it?" Elena's voice interrupted his thoughts.

He stopped next to her.

She handed over the black-and-white photo. He stared at it. This was his baby?

He squinted, trying to make out more than a blob. Try as he might, he didn't see anything that resembled a baby.

"What's the matter?" Elena asked.

"Ah…what?" He wasn't sure what to say that wouldn't get him in more trouble.

"You were frowning when you looked at the sonogram. If you don't want anything to do with the baby, just say so."

Luca shook his head. He decided to leave his uncertainties about his parental abilities unspoken. "It's just that I can't make out the baby. It's just such a…"

"Go ahead. You can say it. It's a blob. I call it my little peanut. That's the gestational sac. It was too early to make out the baby."

"Oh." He sat down on the edge of the bed and gave her the photo. "I thought I was missing something."

"Just relax. We both have a lot to learn."

It was nice to know that he wasn't in this all alone. "I'm really sorry I made such a mess of things today with the wedding and the reception."

She looked at him. "You didn't. It…it was really nice. It just wasn't real."

"But it was real. We are married."

"But not for the right reason." When he went to protest, she pressed a finger to his lips. "Do you love me? Not like a friend, but like a lover with that I-can't-live-without-you passion?"

He wanted to tell her that he did, but he couldn't lie. He never allowed himself to love anyone. Maybe it was his parents' numerous fights behind closed doors—fights they didn't think anyone ever heard. But he had, and he distinctly remembered his mother saying that she wished she'd never married his father.

He'd only been ten, but that night he was certain the world he knew would never be the same. Because his mother did pack her things. She took him and his very young sister and they went to his uncle's. He'd never thought his parents would work it out. But somehow, some way, they did return to his father in Halencia. He never did learn if his mother had married his father out of love or duty.

Or maybe he'd dismissed the idea of love when his mother had been murdered. When he learned that life ended in a split second that you could never be prepared for. He watched his father—the strongest man he'd ever known—disappear within himself and become a shell of the man he'd once been.

If that was love, Luca was certain that he didn't want any part of it.

"No. I'm not in love with you." His voice was soft, as though that would ease the blow.

"Good." Elena blinked repeatedly and swallowed hard.

"Good? I didn't think you'd say that."

"Why not? I've already had one man lie to me. At least you're honest."

He was quiet for a moment as he digested her words. "So you're okay—I mean, you don't have any expectations about us?"

"I expect that we'll do whatever it takes to protect our child."

"Agreed. But earlier—"

"Was pregnancy hormones and exhaustion."

"You're sure?" When she nodded, he said, "Then we should get you home." He got to his feet. "Stay here. I'll be right back."

He strode out of the room. He grabbed his clothes from earlier and changed into them. This evening hadn't ended the way he'd planned—with a fancy dinner including all of Elena's favorite dishes. But he'd never been around a pregnant woman before. In the future, he'd see to it that she didn't overdo it.

Now dressed in shorts and a collared shirt, he returned

to Elena's bedroom. The evening had come to an end. He should feel relieved, but he didn't.

She looked at him, and her eyes momentarily widened. "What happened to your clothes?"

"What?" He glanced down at his outfit. "They look fine to me. And here are yours. Hurry and change. I'll have the car brought round."

Before she could protest, he closed the door and walked away. He strode back to the living room, where he blew out all the candles that adorned the room. This whole evening had gone astray. And now Luca had to face spending his wedding night without his bride.

And try as he might, he couldn't stop thinking of that kiss at the chapel and then the one here at the penthouse. He hadn't married Elena out of love, so what was up with the feelings that had bubbled up inside him when the minister pronounced them husband and wife?

CHAPTER FOURTEEN

WHY HAD HE suddenly gotten so quiet?

Elena sat in the back of the town car as it eased down the private lane to her parents' house. Luca sat beside her, staring out the window. Ever since he'd seen the sonogram, he hadn't said anything about the baby. Was it possible he was having second thoughts about being part of the baby's life?

She wanted to ask him then and there, but she couldn't. She didn't want the driver to overhear.

And then the car pulled to a stop in front of her parents' house. They got out and strolled up the walk. Before they made it to the stoop, Elena stopped and turned to Luca. "Don't forget your promise to keep the marriage and the baby a secret."

"I won't." In the moonlight, Luca looked so handsome. He'd worked so hard to make today memorable, but she'd gone and ruined it. The guilt weighed on her. She would make it up to him. She wasn't sure how just yet, but something would come to her.

Luca cleared his throat. "And now you and that little one need to get some rest."

This was the opening she needed. She swallowed hard as her stomach quivered with nerves. "Do you want the baby?"

His eyes widened in surprise. "I married you, didn't I?"

"Answering my question with a question isn't an answer."

"It's all you're going to get tonight. It's getting late and we're both tired."

"That's it?" Her voice started to rise. "You're dismissing me and my concerns."

Luca shushed her. "We don't want to make a scene. We'll talk later."

"Sometimes you can be the most frustrating man."

He smiled at her like she'd just paid him a compliment. Then Luca swiped aside a strand of her hair and tucked it behind her ear. He leaned toward her. Her heart lodged in her throat as she realized he was going to kiss her. She should turn away and rebuff his attempt to smooth things over. But she couldn't move.

Then his lips pressed to her forehead. Her forehead? Really?

His voice was deep when he said, "I'll see you tomorrow for Annabelle's party."

She didn't respond.

And then her husband retreated to the waiting car.

Elena stood there watching as the car pulled away and the taillights eventually faded into the night. Had today really happened? And then she glanced down. The light along her parents' cobblestone walk reflected off her brand-new diamond ring.

Wondering if Luca had forgotten about his ring, too, she pulled out her phone. She dashed off a quick text. Seconds later, he texted her back.

Thanks for the reminder.

"Elena, is that you?" Her mother's voice came from the doorway.

"Yes, it's me."

"Well, what are you doing lurking around in the dark? Come inside."

Elena slipped the rings from her finger and slid them in her purse. It felt wrong to be hiding them, but how could she explain this to her mother when she couldn't even explain all the conflicting emotions she was experiencing?

Not that her mother gave her much time to think about

the wedding as her mother launched into a series of questions. "Did you talk to the reporters today?"

"How did you know about them?"

"Everyone on the palace grounds knows. What they don't know is what they wanted with you. Lucky for you, the people who live around here aren't up on reading the tabloids. But my friends read them, and I've been fielding calls all day. I don't know what to tell them."

"Tell them the stories are all lies."

"Even the one about you being pregnant—"

"What?"

"Yes, they have photos of you visiting the doctor's office, and some unnamed source let it slip that you're carrying that man's baby."

She wanted to tell her mother the whole truth, but she'd promised Luca to keep this secret for a few more days. And her mother was known for her lack of discretion, which was why her father never talked about his work at home.

"That...that is another fabrication."

Her mother eyed her. "Are you sure?"

"I'm sure that I'm not carrying Steven's baby. It's not even a possibility. Now, I'm tired and I have a busy day tomorrow, so I think I'll turn in—"

"Are you going to Annabelle's party?"

Elena nodded.

"With Luca again?"

"We don't have any plans, but I'm sure we'll run into each other, since I'm a guest and he's the brother of the hostess."

"Have a good time."

"I will. Good night." She made her way to the steps, anxious to get to her room and be alone with her thoughts.

But sleep didn't come easily. She kept replaying the events of the day. She wondered if they had made the right choice to marry. She'd always believed that people should marry for love, and now she'd done the exact opposite.

Because there was definitely no love in the relationship— not the kind that should exist between husband and wife. And she wasn't about to put her scarred heart on the line, especially for a man who'd repeatedly rejected love from those around him. She wondered if he even knew how to love someone.

She knew his mother's death had left a scar on him. It had set him adrift and made him willing to take needless chances with his safety. In fact, she'd worried more than once that his daring stunts of cliff diving and bungee jumping would cost him his life, but he'd made it through that rebellious period with only a couple of broken bones and a bruised ego.

He'd worked so hard to distance himself from his family. She knew what he'd been doing—protecting himself. Because the family that he knew had crumbled.

Was that what he was doing now? Was he holding her at a distance because he was afraid that if he let her in and it didn't work out his life would crumble again? Or did he feel absolutely nothing but friendship for her?

He could do this.

He could pretend he hadn't just married the most beautiful woman in the world.

Thank goodness Elena had thought to text him the night before about his ring, because it had completely slipped his mind. He'd almost blown it, and just after he'd promised Elena that he would keep their marriage under wraps until Sunday, when Annabelle's engagement festivities were officially concluded.

But he had to admit to himself that spending his wedding night alone was a complete and utter downer. He'd never considered marrying, but that didn't mean he didn't understand that the wedding night was supposed to be quite memorable. Instead, he hadn't even gotten a good-night kiss. Was this the sort of future he'd doomed them to?

He recalled their conversation before they said their vows. Elena had made him agree that they wouldn't share a bed. At the time, he'd been so concerned about claiming his son or daughter that he'd have agreed to almost anything. It wasn't until now that he'd realized what this concession truly meant.

He never contemplated what it would be like having a platonic marriage with a woman as beautiful as Elena, both on the inside and out. After all, he was a man. He couldn't just not notice that she was stunning. He wasn't the only one who noticed her rare beauty. She couldn't even walk down the street without men whistling.

But what none of them knew was that she was now his legally and otherwise—although the *otherwise* had a bit of a hitch. His thoughts rolled back to the kiss they'd shared yesterday after the wedding. It had caught him off guard. He'd thought he could do this whole fake marriage thing, but now he was having serious doubts.

"Luca, what are you doing all the way over here?"

He blinked and realized that he'd been totally lost in his thoughts. And then somehow the object of his daydream appeared before him. Elena stood there giving him a strange look.

"What did you say?" he asked.

She waved away his words. "It doesn't matter. You look like you have something on your mind. What is it? Or do I already know?"

"You know?" And then he realized that his voice came out a bit off-key.

She sent him a strange look. "Yes, I know. My mother told me about the latest story in the tabloid. I'll give them this much—they sure don't waste any time in going after a person."

"I take it there was another story about you?"

She nodded. "I thought you knew."

"Um, no. Do you think they went digging up more information on you when you didn't appear at the gate yesterday to answer their questions?"

"Something like that. Apparently they have a photo of me visiting my doctor's office."

"So what does that mean? You can't be the only woman who visits her doctor."

"Apparently they've got an unnamed source in the office, and they told them I was pregnant."

"And your mother knows."

Elena nodded. "But I hedged around her questions. So she doesn't know what's real and what's lies. I hate this."

He took her hand in his and gave it a squeeze. "I know you do. But it's almost over. If you want, we can just tell everyone today."

"The idea is so tempting, but Annabelle is so happy. I don't want to ruin this once-in-a-lifetime experience. Your sister really went all out for this celebration, and I noticed that you two are getting closer."

He nodded. "She's a little less angry with me for being gone all these years."

"So then there's good coming out of this week?"

"I suppose you could say that."

"Then I will put off my mother for a bit longer. If only I could disconnect her internet for the rest of the week, it would certainly help."

"Would you like me to borrow a pair of wire cutters from the palace staff?"

"You have absolutely no idea just how tempting that idea is."

They both laughed. And he couldn't help but stare at her. Her face lit up with happiness. Her eyes twinkled. And once again he felt an odd sensation in his chest—a warmth.

CHAPTER FIFTEEN

European football.

Elena stood on the sidelines and smiled. Thankfully Annabelle had given them a heads-up about today's activities so she could dress appropriately in shorts and a yellow cotton top. It'd been more years than she wanted to count since she'd hit the field, but she did have to admit that she'd played pretty well in her day.

"Okay, everybody, gather round." Annabelle waved everyone over. "What should we do? Pick two captains and let them choose teams? Or should we play guys on girls?"

The second option definitely got more votes from the women. But the men were shockingly quiet.

"Well, it seems it's a draw." She turned back to Grayson, and they whispered back and forth for a minute. Then he handed her something. "Okay. Since it's a tie, we're going to toss for it. Heads we do coed. Tails we do boys versus girls."

Annabelle flipped the coin high in the air. It turned end over end, reflecting the sunlight in the process. She caught it and looked up with a smile. "Looks like it's coed. Now for captains. Let's see."

"You and Grayson should be captains, since it's your party," one guest interjected.

Elena liked the idea. "Yeah, go for it."

As more and more people cheered on the idea, Annabelle waved her hands, trying to silence everyone. "I hate to disappoint everyone, but I'm not playing. As most of you know, I'm not coordinated in the least. So I'm going to be the cheer squad." She rushed over to a chair a few feet behind her and grabbed two little white pom-poms. She shook them and smiled broadly. "I came prepared. In my place, I elect Elena."

Elena couldn't help but smile. She liked that after all these years, Luca's sister still thought so highly of her. And since they were now family, it would certainly help matters.

But Elena thought of her condition—she didn't think playing football with the guys was such a good idea. One misplaced ball could hit her abdomen. But how in the world did she gracefully back out without upsetting Annabelle?

Annabelle gestured for Elena to step up beside her. Maybe it'd be possible to coach from the sidelines. That sounded like a good plan. If anyone said anything, she'd blame her lack of activity on her job and not wanting to return with a black eye or broken nose.

Elena took her place next to Annabelle. It was then that she noticed Luca. He was staring directly at her with a distinct frown. What had she done now?

She glanced away, hoping no one would notice his odd behavior. If he didn't lighten up, people were going to start suspecting that something was up between them.

Annabelle took both Elena's and Grayson's hands and raised them above her head. "Okay, these are your captains. And just like when we were kids, they are going to take turns picking players. Good luck—"

"Wait a second," Luca said. "I don't think that's a good idea."

Annabelle's smile faded. "What? The game?"

"No," Luca said, approaching them. "I don't think Elena should play football."

Annabelle's forehead creased. "Is there something we don't know?"

Elena knew what he was up to, and she didn't like it. Her hands balled up at her sides. They might be married now, but she could take care of herself and their baby. Perhaps it was time they laid out some understandings about this nontraditional arrangement.

Not about to let Luca make a scene, Elena spoke up.

"What's the matter, Luca? Are you afraid that I'll beat you like when we were kids?"

"No, I was thinking that you might not want the ball hitting you. You know, to the stomach or, worse, the face. A broken nose probably won't help your career."

They might be thinking along the same lines, but that didn't mean she was going to let him tell her what to do. "And that's why I was planning to coach from the sidelines."

"Or you can keep me company." Annabelle gave her a hopeful look. "I'll share my pom-poms with you."

Before Elena could respond, Grayson spoke up. "Actually, this will work out. As it was, we were going to have an extra person. Now the teams will be equal."

"What do you say?" Annabelle asked.

"Looks like I'll be joining the cheering section." Elena refused to look at Luca.

Annabelle glanced around. "And now I need a replacement captain. Luca, since you caused the ruckus, you can be the captain. Get over here and start picking players. We have a game to play."

Elena joined Annabelle off to the side of the field that had been painted up with white lines just like a regulation field. Even nets stood at either end. And the part Elena liked best was the hot dog and refreshment cart. She was getting a little hungry...and since she was eating for two now, she had the perfect excuse to ditch her diet for the day.

"So what's up with you and my brother?" Annabelle took a seat in one of the fold-out chairs.

Elena sat next to her. She willed herself to act normal. "Not much."

"Sure seems like something to me. The looks you two were sending each other were rather stormy. I hope you two aren't fighting. You barely see each other anymore."

"Oh, we're not fighting. I promise." At least not yet—not until she was alone with Luca.

"You're sure? Because I could say something to him. Now that my brother has reemerged into our lives, he seems to think he knows what's best for everyone. Don't let him push you around."

"Trust me, I've known him long enough to know all his tricks."

"Good." Annabelle smiled. "Us girls, we have to stick together."

"Yes, we do."

Was it wrong that Elena was starting to feel like she would have an ally in Annabelle? Her friend didn't even know the truth yet. Would Annabelle be upset when she learned that her brother had eloped? Would everyone think that he had married beneath himself?

Elena lifted her chin a little higher. She was, after all, famous. That had to count for something. She would make sure people respected her, starting with her husband.

"What was that back there?"

The hiss in Elena's voice drew Luca up short.

He stopped on the beach and glanced around to make sure they were alone. They'd meandered toward the beach while everyone else headed back to the palace to get cleaned up before dinner. But right now, food was the last thing on Luca's mind.

He turned back to her. "What are you talking about?"

"That scene you made before the football game. You shouldn't have done it."

"Well, excuse me for worrying about my—" he caught himself before he said *wife* "—my child. I was just doing what I thought was best."

"That's not for you to do. I can take care of myself. I was about to back out of playing the game before you interrupted."

"I didn't know." He suddenly felt as though he'd done

something wrong when all he'd meant to do was make sure that everyone was safe. Being a husband and father was trickier than he'd imagined.

"I think the problem is that we rushed into this marriage and we didn't take time to figure out how it was going to work."

He had a distinct feeling he wasn't going to like what she said next. "And how do you think it should work?"

"Well, my life is in Paris. I plan to return there."

He didn't like the thought of her being so far away. "When do you plan to leave?"

"My flight is scheduled for next week."

He nodded, but he didn't speak right away. Time was running out for them. He took a moment before he spoke. He'd already learned the value of carefully considering his words where Elena was concerned. "You do realize the paparazzi is going to follow you around and dig up whatever dirt they can find?"

She shrugged it off, but he caught a glimpse of the worry in her eyes. She didn't like living her life in the spotlight. So why was she in such a rush to get back to that world? Was it truly her career? Or was she anxious to get away from him?

"How will you work? Soon you'll be showing."

She said something, but it was so soft that he couldn't quite catch it. "What did you say?"

"I was fired."

"I'm sorry. I didn't know." And then another thought came to him. "So this means you don't have to leave?"

"I've been hoping to work in another area of the fashion industry. Something behind the scenes. So my pregnancy won't be an issue."

His hopes were dashed. "And this work, it's that important to you?"

She nodded, but her gaze didn't quite meet his. "I'm

being mentored by Francois Lacroix, one of the greatest fashion designers in the world."

When she mentioned the name, Luca was surprised. Even he had heard of the man. As she talked about this new endeavor, she became animated. Her face lit up and it was obvious that she'd found something that brought her tremendous joy.

Luca could see why this was important to her. "He must see a lot of promise in you. I'd like to see your designs."

Elena's blue eyes widened. "You would?"

"Sure. I think it's great that you are doing something you're passionate about."

"I don't know why I was worried that you'd try to talk me out of it. You always supported me, even when everyone else washed their hands. Like when I wanted to test out of school early so I could move to Paris."

"How could I tell you to stay put when I didn't?"

"But it was more than that. You always told me that I could do whatever I put my mind to. Unlike my mother, who thought I should stay close to home and find a suitable husband. She never did understand my need to venture into the world and find my place."

"So you're really happy in Paris?" He braced himself for her answer.

"I am happy. I don't know if it's Paris or the fact that I'm chasing my dreams. Can you imagine, instead of me modeling someone else's clothes, one day it might be my name up there and someone else might be wearing my fashions?" A broad smile lit up her face.

He didn't want to stand between Elena and that happiness. But they did have a marriage and a baby to consider. That had to be their priority. Surely she'd agree.

"And what of the baby and our marriage?" he asked.

"I gave it some thought last night, and I think I have a compromise of sorts."

"I'm listening." He doubted he'd like this suggestion, because it probably had to do with Paris.

"I think you and I should stay married for the next year. By then the baby will be born, and we can decide whether to continue the marriage, or if either of us wants out, we can end it."

Well, that sounded good so far. "I think that's agreeable."

"As for the living arrangement, I'll be spending the bulk of my time in Paris, and I'm sure you'll be spending most of your time in Halencia."

"No."

"What do you mean, no? You won't be staying in Halencia?"

"No, we aren't going to live apart."

She frowned. "Of course we are. We can visit each other on holidays. This doesn't have to change things between us unless we let it."

His jaw tensed. It had already changed everything. As soon as he said, "I do," his whole world seemed to shift, and he had yet to regain his footing. "And the baby? Am I never supposed to see it, either?"

"You're impossible to talk to when you're angry." She turned and started to walk away.

He reached out, catching her wrist. "Elena, don't walk away. We need to get this all out there. What about the baby?"

She sighed and turned. "He or she will live with me in Paris. You can visit as much as you like."

"And that's it?" he ground out between clenched teeth. "I'm just going to be the absentee father?"

She moved the sand around with her foot. "I thought about it, and I just don't see any other alternative—at least not until the child is older."

"And by then I'll be a stranger to them." His voice was filled with anger. He hadn't even realized until this moment just how passionate he was about playing an important role in his child's life. "Is that what you want?"

"I…I don't know. What else can we do?"

At this point, he was the one to turn and walk away. He had to put distance between them, because he didn't trust himself to pick the right words in the heat of the moment.

Didn't Elena understand what she was asking of him?

Sure, maybe he'd never expected to be a father, but that choice had been taken out of his hands. And now, well, he was starting to imagine a little boy, inquisitive and daring, or a little girl with her mother's forget-me-not blue eyes and blond locks. He was starting to put images to the concept of Elena being pregnant. With each passing day, it was becoming more of a reality to him.

And he wanted to do more for his child than give them his name. But now Elena was blocking him from doing that. She'd essentially written him out of her life as well as the baby's. Now what was he going to do about it?

He'd really mucked things up.

Later that evening, Luca sat at the enormous wooden desk in the palace library. The remainder of the lemon grove's financial reports had shown up while he was out. Now it was his job to formulate a plan to salvage his legacy. He needed to turn things around. He just couldn't fail his family again.

But instead of figures and projections, all he could think about right now was Elena. After telling himself that he'd keep his cool and watch what he said, he'd blown it. He just couldn't stand the thought of not playing a vital role in his child's life. That fact should shock him after telling himself for years that he wouldn't have a family, but instead the decision to be an active part of his child's life came easily to him—as natural as breathing.

And for Elena to try to cut him out of that experience

was unthinkable. He'd thought he knew her, but perhaps he was mistaken. Could that be right? Was Elena really a stranger to him?

"How does it look?" his father asked as he strode into the room.

Torn from his thoughts, Luca glanced up. "Are you sure this is everything?"

"Of course. Why? What are you missing?"

"Profits. And your debt ratio is astronomical."

His father's face was pale and drawn. As he looked at his father, Luca could see the toll the years had taken on the duke. He didn't look good. Luca truly had been gone too long. It had been easier to be secluded from his family than to have to deal with all the problems and responsibilities family entailed—like the problems facing him now.

But those days were over. If he were honest with himself, that decision had been made when his sister invited him back to Mirraccino for this celebration. He hadn't fully realized it then, but where he normally avoided family gatherings, he was drawn to this one. Of course, that might have had something to do with the fact that his sister had also told him that Elena had been invited.

Luca just never imagined that he would arrive to find out that his father was in such deep financial trouble. It would be a miracle if they'd be able to keep their home.

His father pulled a wooden chair next to the desk and settled on it. "I tried. It just got away from me. I thought I could turn things around."

Luca focused on the summary spreadsheet that he'd created on his laptop. "I've done an overview of your debt, expenses and revenue. Without a major influx of cash, I don't see being able to turn things around." When he glanced over at his father, he caught him blinking repeatedly. This display of emotion from his stalwart father shook Luca to the core. "I'm sorry."

His father sniffed back the rush of emotions. "You have nothing to be sorry for. I am to blame."

"I should have come back sooner instead of letting you deal with it all on your own."

"What can we do?"

Luca leaned back in his chair and rubbed his jaw. "I'll be honest—it isn't good. If you were one of my clients, I'd tell you to sell everything, make settlements with your creditors and start over."

"But our home—I couldn't bear to lose it. It's full of memories..."

Of Luca's mother? Was it possible that his parents cared more for each other than he would ever know? Perhaps relationships were more complicated than he'd imagined. He was certainly learning that with Elena.

"Can I ask you something?" Luca uttered the words before he evaluated the ramifications of what he was about to ask.

"Sure. You know that you can talk to me about anything."

Luca had never felt that way about his father, but perhaps the years and loneliness had mellowed the man. "It's about Mother."

"What about her?"

"Did you ever love her?"

His father leaned back as though the question struck him physically. "Why would you ask such a thing?"

This was where it got difficult. Luca swallowed hard. "I heard you two. When I was little, you would fight, a lot. Annabelle was too young to remember, but I do. I remember Mother saying that she wished you two hadn't married."

His father's shoulders drooped. "I'm sorry you overheard us. We thought that we were being discreet." His father took a moment as though to sort through his memories. "Your mother and I were practically strangers when we married.

It was arranged to strengthen alliances between Halencia and Mirraccino and it took us a long time to find common ground. With each passing year, our respect for each other grew, as did our friendship. It was hard won, which I like to think made our relationship stronger."

"Why did I never know any of this?"

His father shrugged. "I guess you never asked and I never thought of it."

"But you two ended up loving each other?"

"How could I not love your mother? She was the most amazing woman I'd ever met. She was gracious and kind, not to mention a beauty. But she had a strong spirit and was quite determined to do things her way. There were numerous areas where we had different views, including her allegiance to her brother, the king. That's what most of our heated exchanges were about. But what you heard were words spoken in the heat of the moment. What you didn't hear were the apologies."

Luca couldn't quite digest all this information. He wasn't sure what to make of it. His parents' story certainly wasn't like the fairy tales. Theirs was complicated and messy.

And Luca didn't do messy.

"Thank you for telling me," Luca said.

"I hope it helps you."

Luca wondered if his father knew more than he was saying, but Luca wasn't going there. They had another matter to discuss.

"I've gone over these numbers for the past few hours, and at this point, I know that if something isn't done right away, you'll lose everything." He took a deep breath. "I have some money set aside, which, along with my trust fund, we can use to pay off some of the more pressing debts, but it still won't be enough to make the company solvent. However, it should give us some breathing room."

"You…you would do that?"

"Why do you sound surprised? This is my legacy and that of my children. I want to hold on to it as much as you."

"Children?" There was a hint of glee in his father's voice. "Does this mean you've decided to settle down with a family?"

Avoiding the question, Luca said, "It means I have a vested interest in making this work. And it means I need to step up my efforts to bring in a new revenue source, and I think I know of a way."

The answer was the king. He had connections far beyond the normal businessman. In fact, the Mirraccino palace in many instances acted as an agent for its citizens. Now, granted, the lemon grove was not part of Mirraccino, but they were family. Luca could only hope that the king did better by his extended family than Luca had done by his immediate family. Guilt weighed heavy on his shoulders for pushing away his family and ignoring his obligations after his mother's death.

Everything was now in jeopardy—his tenuous relationship with his father and his sister as well as the lemon grove. He had to hope that if he fixed the business then his relationships would continue to fall into place. But how could he get to the king when he was sequestered behind guarded doors?

Elena's image came to mind. Her father was the only person the king had been seeing since the truth of Luca's mother's murder had been revealed. The news had hit the king especially hard, since Luca's mother had been trying to protect him from one of his own trusted employees.

Luca dismissed the idea of involving Elena. It didn't feel right. Besides, with the way they'd left things, she wouldn't be in any frame of mind to help him. There had to be another way.

CHAPTER SIXTEEN

THERE WAS NO avoiding this evening's festivities.

As it was, Elena had pleaded a headache the day before and stayed home, missing out on the croquet and bocce ball tournaments. She had been looking forward to them, too, because they were activities she could do and not worry about the baby. She had to admit that she did have a bit of a competitive streak.

But she knew that Luca was upset with her. In fact, their last conversation had been the angriest she'd ever seen him. He was usually so laid-back and let things roll off his shoulders. But this thing with the baby—it really got to him.

Was it possible the self-proclaimed bachelor was more excited to be a father than he was willing to admit? If so, it would be the first sign that Luca was letting his guard down. Was it possible? Or was she only seeing what she wanted to see?

Elena rushed around her bedroom in her parents' home. Tonight was a dinner and dance that would wrap up the weeklong celebration. This morning Annabelle had phoned to check on her and make sure that Elena would be in attendance for the evening's festivities.

Knock. Knock.

"Dear, are you almost ready?" Her mother's voice echoed through the closed door.

"Almost."

"I just don't want you to be late. And the car is here—"

"What car?" Elena rushed to the window.

Was Luca out there waiting for her? Her stomach quivered with nerves. They'd left things in such an awkward spot that she wasn't sure what to say to him. She had no answers, just more questions.

"I assume Annabelle sent it for you."

Not Luca. Okay. "I'll be down in a jiff."

"Do you need any help?"

"No. Thanks. I've got it." She rushed back to the full-length mirror.

Tonight she was wearing another one of her own creations. It was a light blue material. The shade was similar to her eyes, or so she'd been told. It had a strapless beaded bustier and attached to it was a long chiffon skirt in the same shade. It wasn't one of her more daring designs, but this was, after all, an appearance at the palace. Traditional trumped experimental in this particular scenario.

She wondered if Luca would like it. He had no idea that she was going to wear an Elena Ricci original. But on second thought, her clothes would probably be the last thing on his mind tonight. She'd hoped that he would have calmed down enough to call her by now, but there was still no word from him.

She slipped on white sandals that strapped over her pink-painted toes and wrapped around her ankles. She pulled up the zipper in the back of each shoe. When she grabbed her clutch purse from the bed, it was time to put on a show.

With each step, her nerves became more taut. She had no idea what to say to Luca, and there was no avoiding him this evening. She truly wanted to make things better between them. Their marriage had barely made it twenty-four hours before they'd had their first major fight. If she believed in omens, this would be a worrisome one.

The clap of hands had her gazing at the bottom of the steps. There stood not only her mother but also her father.

"Father, what are you doing here? Shouldn't you be with the king?"

"Your mother told me you were getting all dressed up tonight and I couldn't miss it."

She rushed over and gave him a kiss on the cheek and a

hug. She loved her father. He might not have been around as much as she'd wanted, but when he was there, he was alert and attentive.

And then she turned to her mother, who now had tears in her eyes. They hugged. Her mother might be difficult, but her heart was always in the right place.

As Elena made her way out the door, she realized her child deserved a loving home just like that, not a home filled with heated words or, worse, stony silence because the parents were frustrated with having to give up their dreams. If she couldn't find a way to build a genuine marriage with Luca, she knew she'd have to end things. Otherwise, it wouldn't be fair to any of them.

This acknowledgment hit her in the chest, knocking the air from her lungs. What would happen to Luca if she walked away? In the end, would he be relieved?

She halted the disturbing thoughts. She was jumping too far ahead. First, they had to get through this evening, and considering where they'd left things, it would be a challenge.

The car ride to the palace was short, and in no time she was being ushered inside. The grand dining room was set for the party. The table was the longest Elena had ever seen in her life—it would easily accommodate fifty.

Elena had only been in this room once. She had been quite small, and she and Luca had been sneaking around the palace. The room had been opened up for cleaning, and she had been floored by its vastness. She knew instantly that she didn't belong there, but it didn't stop her from having a quick look around. She had been a curious kid, anxious to find out what she'd been missing out on.

Now as an adult, she was still awed by the room and its elegance. The room was decorated in red brocade wallpaper. On each wall were portraits of family ancestors. Crystal chandeliers lined the long table.

And once again, she didn't feel as though she belonged in this room with royalty, statesmen and dignitaries. Even if she had known them when they would play in the flower gardens and swim in the sea, she wasn't one of them. Even with her secret marriage to Luca, she didn't feel like a member of this prestigious group.

It looked like everyone had arrived. They were all standing off to the side of the table in small groups, enjoying wine and appetizers served by the staff. They were done reliving some of the highlights of their childhood. Tonight they were all elegantly dressed adults, here to honor Annabelle and her soon-to-be husband.

Elena was so relieved that she and Luca had kept the scandal, the elopement and the baby all under wraps. After tonight, they wouldn't have to keep choking down the truth. They could be themselves, and maybe once the pressure was off they could figure out what the future held for them.

She scanned the room, but Luca was nowhere to be found. How could that be? This was his sister's party. He wouldn't miss it, not now that he was trying to make up for the past.

"There you are." Annabelle rushed over. Her off-white gown was figure fitting and accentuated all her attributes. She looked stunning.

"Sorry. I didn't think I was late."

"You aren't. Everyone just wants to get an early start on the evening." Annabelle gave her a worried look. "Are you feeling better?"

"Yes." Elena felt the heat swirl in her chest and rush to her cheeks. "I'm really sorry about yesterday. I just wasn't up for a day in the sun."

"I understand. With headaches, the bright light is the worst." Annabelle took her by the arm and led her over toward a cluster of people. "Let's get you a drink."

"Actually, I was going to ask you if Luca is coming this evening."

Annabelle glanced around. "He should be here. I know that he had an important meeting earlier, but he promised that he would be here. I'll go find him."

"No, let me."

Annabelle nodded. "But don't you go and get lost, too."

"I won't. I promise."

Perhaps it was best she met up with Luca away from prying eyes. She had no idea how it would go, because she'd never been in such a serious situation with Luca before.

She hoped they could find a way to smile and get through the evening. Just tonight and they would have made Annabelle's celebration perfect.

She started for the door when Luca stepped inside. Elena stopped in her tracks. She observed the frown on his face and the way his eyes were full of turmoil.

Oh, no! This was not good. Not good at all.

The situation was dire.

More so than Luca first thought.

How in the world was he supposed to convince Elena to stay with him in Halencia now? There was no way he could provide her with the life she would expect and deserve, not unless there was a miracle. The only thing he did know was that the news could wait until tomorrow.

Luca tugged at the collar of his white dress shirt. This was the last place he wanted to be. He did not like tuxes. They were stuffy and uncomfortable. They had to have been created by a woman, because he couldn't imagine a man designing something so miserably uncomfortable.

He hadn't even worn a tux to his own wedding. So when his sister insisted that he wear one this evening, he'd almost blurted out about the wedding. But he caught himself in time. So the only reason he was wearing this monkey suit was to appease his sister and possibly Elena.

He'd really messed things up on the beach the other day.

He'd lost his cool, and she'd been avoiding him since then. He'd thought of calling her, but what they needed to say to each other was better said in person.

And then his gaze latched on to Elena. She was standing there in a beautiful dress, but it was the expression on her face that made the breath catch in the back of his throat. She was staring at him with a lost look on her face. She was looking at him like he was a stranger. The knowledge dug at him.

They approached each other, their gazes never wavering.

At the same time, they said, "We need to talk."

"There you are, brother. I was worried you got caught up in something and forgot the time." Annabelle rushed up to them.

"I could never forget you," he said and forced a smile.

"Good. It's time to sit down." Annabelle pointed to the table.

"So much for talking," Luca whispered in Elena's ear.

He knew his sister had done a formal seating chart, which meant he wouldn't be seated next to Elena. She would probably be at one end while he was seated at the other with a chatty woman next to him. Tonight he wasn't in the mood to make light conversation.

When Luca started searching out his seat, his sister said, "You're up here, next to me." And then before he could ask, Annabelle said, "And Elena is right next to you."

That was very unorthodox, and his sister always maintained formality at these occasions. She was up to something, but he was so off lately that he couldn't put his finger on exactly what his sister had planned.

Annabelle clinked her glass. "Everyone, please have a seat."

It took a few minutes until everyone was seated. It was then that Luca noticed there were three empty seats—all directly across from him. What was she doing?

Annabelle remained standing. "I have a few more guests."

Through a side door Elena's mother entered, followed by both of their fathers. Oh, no. They were so busted. He didn't dare look at Elena. He could already feel her gaze boring into the back of his head.

Annabelle started speaking with a very serious expression. "Ladies and gentlemen, thank you all for coming." As she kept talking, she gave him and Elena some strange looks. "I'm thankful that my big brother is home with his family. And if the news I've uncovered is any indication, I think he'll be spending more time here."

A murmur rippled around the table.

His father sent him a questioning look, but Luca pretended not to notice. This was not good. Not good at all. The parents hadn't even been clued in and here was his sister about to blow the whistle in front of the whole family and their closest friends.

It was like watching a crash in slow motion and being too stunned to act. His sister was standing there smiling and getting ready to reveal their secret marriage. How was everyone going to react?

CHAPTER SEVENTEEN

THIS WAS GOING to be a disaster.

Elena lowered her gaze as Annabelle continued to address the guests. Why was she doing this? Had Luca told her? Elena couldn't believe he would tell his sister without mentioning it to her, but obviously someone had told her about the marriage.

And then Elena wondered just how much Annabelle knew. Did she know about the baby? *Please don't let her blurt that out.* Elena really wanted to tell her parents when the time was right. They deserved to know first.

"It has come to my attention that my big brother has been keeping a rather large secret from us," Annabelle said.

All eyes trained on Luca, followed by the murmur of voices. Everyone was trying to guess the news. But they were never going to guess that they'd eloped.

Heat engulfed Elena's chest, neck and face. If Annabelle was trying to punish them for keeping this secret, she was doing a good job. If only Elena could fade into the woodwork, she would—in a heartbeat.

Luca glanced at her. Her gaze searched his to find out if he'd known his sister was going to do this. As though he could read her thoughts, his brows rose and he gave a slight shrug.

Great! Annabelle was running loose. And who knew what she was going to say. Elena reached out for Luca's hand. They were in this together. He squeezed her hand, but the reassuring gesture did nothing to settle her queasy stomach.

Annabelle continued, "And now for the news that has come to light." She paused as though for dramatic effect. "My brother and the lovely Elena have eloped."

Gasps ensued around the table.

Elena chanced a glance at her mother, who was all smiles. Thank goodness! At least one person was happy for them. Elena wasn't sure whether Annabelle was happy or angry. Not that she would blame Annabelle for being upset. This was supposed to be her time in the limelight.

Annabelle said, "Tonight's celebration has turned into a wedding supper and reception in the ballroom." She turned to them. "Come on now, stand up, you two. You surely didn't think you were going to get away with this, did you?"

Neither of them answered. They just held on to each other's hands.

"Ladies and gentlemen, please allow me to introduce my brother, the Earl of Halencia, and his wife, Elena."

Everyone clapped and smiled, including all the parents and most of all Annabelle, who rushed over to hug Luca.

And then she moved to stand in front of Elena. "I can't believe you kept this a secret."

What was she supposed to say to that? "I'm sorry."

"Don't be. If you're happy with my stubborn brother, then more power to you." Annabelle smiled broadly and held out her arms. "Welcome to the family, sis."

"Thank you."

Elena hugged her back. But she couldn't help wondering if this was all for real or if Annabelle was trying to make the best of an awkward situation. Maybe in the rush to the altar, they should have given more thought to their families. Suddenly Elena felt very guilty for leaving them all out of it.

There were hugs all around with the parents and words of congratulations exchanged. Everyone seemed to be taking the news well.

Before the rest of the guests could congratulate them, the staff arrived with trays of food. Everyone took their seats to make things easier for the waitstaff.

Luca leaned over to Elena. "Did you know about this?"

"I had no idea. So how did your sister find out?"

"I don't know, but I intend to find out." He leaned over to his sister. "So how exactly did you find out the news?"

Elena, curious to know the answer herself, leaned closer.

"You mean besides you two acting rather oddly?" When Luca frowned, his sister continued, "Well, there was a delivery for you from the courthouse. I happened to be in the foyer at the time. So I signed for it."

"You read my mail?" Luca asked.

"No. But I do have eyes, and I read the return address. It wasn't hard to put two and two together. With a little research, I had confirmation. It would have been nice if you'd told me."

"We were trying not to ruin your big week."

"You didn't ruin it. I couldn't be happier to know that you are settling down, and with the one person in the world I've always thought was made for you." Annabelle reached out and squeezed his arm.

"Thanks, sis."

Elena blinked repeatedly, hoping to keep her makeup from smearing. She had no idea that his sister's opinion of their marriage would hit her so emotionally. These pregnancy hormones were going to turn her into a crier if she wasn't careful.

When Annabelle's gaze met hers, Elena mouthed a big thank-you.

All the while Luca continued to hold her hand. And it was like a weight had been lifted from her shoulders. Now if only everyone was excited about the baby, but that would wait for another time.

His sister hadn't been kidding.

Luca was impressed. Somehow in such a short amount of time, she'd thrown together a beautiful reception. There was a receiving line, where he and Elena were given best wishes by everyone. Hugs abounded, including another from his father. Two hugs in one night was a record for sure. Maybe the years *had* mellowed his father.

Small tables with white tablecloths surrounded the dance floor. Each table had candles as well as pink, purple and white flower centerpieces. Purple, blue and pink spotlights added a fun vibe to the room. Luca wasn't much for decorations and weddings, but he was touched that his sister had gone to so much trouble for them.

There was only one thing missing from this impressive event—his uncle, the king. It saddened Luca to know that the king was so distraught over events that were not his fault. Still, it was the king's lord-in-waiting who had not only been a spy, but had also murdered the king's sister—Luca's mother.

The king had taken the responsibility for the horrific event personally. His dubious health had declined even further, and he remained sequestered, only dealing with his secretary—Elena's father. It was a sad state of affairs, but Luca refused to let it ruin this moment.

In the background, a live band played. His sister insisted that he and Elena have the first dance. With so many people watching them, it wasn't nearly as intimate as the dance on their wedding night.

He glanced down at Elena, who was suspiciously quiet as they moved around the dance floor. A frown pulled at her lips, but when she noticed that he was looking at her, it disappeared.

"Is everything all right?" he asked. "I mean, you are feeling all right, aren't you?"

"Yes. Why do you ask?"

"Just checking. I'm not used to being around a pregnant woman. So if there's anything you need or want, let me know."

"I will."

They continued dancing. He glanced around at the people and the decorations. "Can you believe my sister went to all this trouble?"

"It's beautiful. But I feel bad that we ruined the last night of her festivities."

"You have to admit that we did try our best to keep a lid on the news. And we almost pulled it off. Don't worry. She's really happy for us."

"I'm glad."

"Then why aren't you smiling?"

A smile blossomed on Elena's very kissable lips, but it didn't quite reach her eyes. Something was bothering her, but this wasn't the time to delve into it.

When the dance concluded, they were about to leave the dance floor when his sister started to chant, "Kiss. Kiss. Kiss."

It didn't take long until everyone joined in, cheering them on.

His gaze moved to Elena's. "Shall we?"

Elena's cheeks took on a rosy hue. Her gaze met and held his. She looked so beautiful, and she was his wife—a concept he was still getting used to. And then she nodded.

He pulled her close and claimed her lips. They were sweet like the berries they'd enjoyed at dinner. And though her kiss was reserved at first, it didn't take long until her arms slipped up around his neck and her lips met his move for move.

Oh, yeah, there are definitely some amazing perks to this fake marriage.

The whistles and applause brought him back to earth. With great reluctance, he released her. Elena's gaze met his once more, and he could see that the kiss had gotten to her as much as it had him. But where did that leave them?

Her life was in Paris. She'd made that abundantly clear.

And he had nothing to offer her—he was about to lose his legacy to creditors. The future looked dismal at best.

At that point, they moved off the dance area to make room for the other couples to take a spin around the floor. Elena's mother came over to speak with her daughter at the same time as his cousins, the twin princes, came over to congratulate him.

Soon the conversation turned to sports. Their group expanded with more men, all giving their thoughts about the upcoming European football season. As usual with this group, opinions were plenty and the conversation was heated. Some things hadn't changed, no matter how much time Luca had been away.

He had no idea how much time passed before he broke away to find his beautiful bride. He'd looked everywhere for Elena. He even asked his sister to check in the ladies' room, but there was no sign of her. Was it possible she'd left her own reception?

He was just about to give up when he noticed that the door to the balcony was slightly ajar. He moved to close it when he noticed a figure in the moonlight standing at the far end that overlooked the gardens.

He stepped outside to get a better look and then realized it was indeed his bride. She hadn't left him after all. A smile pulled at his lips.

He started across the balcony. When he got closer, he noticed that she was frowning again. It was the same look he'd caught on her face earlier when she didn't think anyone was looking. Something serious was on her mind, and he needed to know what it was so he could fix it. It just wasn't right that the bride wasn't having a good time at her own reception.

Even for tonight, he'd set aside his massive problems with the lemon grove and dealing with his father. There was no point in letting them ruin this evening, since there was nothing he could do tonight to change their situation. He just had to hope that tomorrow would bring him the answers he needed.

He made his way across the balcony to Elena's side. "What are you thinking?"

"Nothing."

He didn't believe her for one moment. "It is definitely something."

She turned to him. "Do you really want to know?"

He nodded, because he didn't have a clue why she was upset. Everything had gone so well tonight. Everyone was happy for them. They should be celebrating that their plan was working out.

"You. Me. Us. This phony marriage."

"What about it?" When she didn't immediately respond, he said, "If you don't talk to me, there's no way I can help."

She licked her lips. "I…I've been an outcast my whole life—"

"What are you talking about?"

"I'm talking about growing up here, on the royal grounds. I was never a real part of you and all your cousins. Sure, I got to live here and it was amazing, but I always felt like I was on the outside looking in."

"That's not how any of us saw it. You were always one of us."

"No, I wasn't. I was the daughter of the help."

"You were more than that and you know it." He reached out to her, but she backed away. "We included you in everything."

Elena shook her head. She clearly remembered all the formal events, dinners and parties she had been forbidden to attend. "Not everything."

"Those other occasions weren't important—"

"Maybe not to you, but they were to me. While you and

your sister and cousins were all getting dressed up for a fancy party, I was left alone. I was the only one not invited."

"I'm sorry. You know I would have included you if I could have." Luca frowned. "But I don't understand. That was all a very long time ago. What does any of this have to do with our marriage?"

"I'm getting to that. After feeling like an outsider my entire childhood, I will not be left on the outside of our marriage."

"What's that supposed to mean?"

"That if you can't open up and tell me how you feel about the baby, I can't do this."

What did she mean, she couldn't do this? He was too afraid to ask. He didn't even understand what had brought this on, but he refused to let his marriage fall apart at their reception. That just seemed epically wrong.

"Elena, I do open up to you, as much as I open up to anyone."

"But that's the thing—you don't. You play everything close to the vest. I don't even know if you're going to let down your guard and love our baby."

"Luca, is that you?" Annabelle called out. She came closer. "Oh, Elena, this is where you've been. Somebody we both know—" she nodded toward Luca "—got worried when he couldn't find you."

"Sorry," Elena said. "I just needed a little fresh air."

"No problem. But as soon as you two are ready, it's time to cut the cake."

"We'll be right there," Luca said. He waited until his sister walked away and then he said, "Elena, I know you want a lot from me, and I'm trying my best. Just give me a little time."

"What makes you think that time will help?"

"This does." He leaned forward and pressed his lips to hers.

When they kissed, everything seemed right in the world. There was no need for words. Problems got lost in the haze. There was just him and her, lost in the moment. Lip to lip. Heart to heart. If only life could be so simple.

CHAPTER EIGHTEEN

WHAT ARE WE supposed to do now?

Elena looked at Luca, who was wearing a bewildered expression that must have matched hers. They stood just outside one of the elaborate guesthouses on the estate. They were secluded.

Just the two of them.

And now they would have to talk.

They stood there for a moment in the dark with the stars twinkling overhead. In any other scenario, this would be so romantic. But what their families didn't know was that Luca was not in love with her.

"Shall we go inside?" he asked.

She nodded. "It's late and I'm tired."

In the next moment, she was swept off her feet.

"Luca, you don't have to do this. There aren't any photographers around this time." And then she had second thoughts about her assumption. "Are there?"

"Why are you asking me? I didn't plan this."

And then Elena realized that Annabelle had planned this special evening. And that could only mean one thing— Annabelle approved of the marriage. At last Elena felt as though she'd been accepted. She was one of them—for however long it lasted.

Luca arched a brow. "And what has you smiling?"

Elena realized that she was indeed smiling. She shrugged and then went with the moment. She wrapped her arms around his neck as he carried her into their temporary home. They had been explicitly told that they were to stay put until Monday—or longer if they liked.

"What's up with you?" she asked.

"Me? Why does something have to be up?"

"Because you've been acting surprisingly happy tonight."

"And the problem with that is?"

"The last time I saw you, we'd argued and you'd walked away mad."

"Maybe I had time to cool off and regret walking away."

What was he saying? She wasn't quite sure. But as he carried her into the cozy cottage, she noticed the soft, jazzy tunes filling the air. Her gaze scanned the dimly lit room. Candles were scattered about, from the mantel of the fireplace to the coffee table. The French doors stood wide open with the gentle breeze off the sea rushing into the room.

Elena wasn't sure she wanted to ruin this moment with any serious conversation. Perhaps the reality of their situation could wait until tomorrow. After all the effort that had gone into this setup, it'd be a shame not to enjoy it.

She leaned close to his neck, brushing her lips gently across his skin. Mmm...he smelled like soap combined with his own manly scent. She breathed in deeper.

"What are you doing?" he asked.

"Smelling you."

"What?"

She couldn't help but smile at his startled tone. "You smell good." She leaned in close again. "Really good."

He lowered her feet to the ground. "It's probably best if you don't do that again."

But her arms were still looped around his neck, and she didn't feel like letting go. Maybe it was all the romantic songs that had filled the ballroom. Or maybe it was dancing with him most of the evening and staring into his eyes. Whatever it was, she was going with it.

"Loosen up. This is our wedding night do-over."

"We can't have a do-over." He loosened her arms from his neck and walked over to the open French doors.

"Sure we can—"

"A do-over implies that we had a first wedding night. And I distinctly recall spending that night alone. Remember?" He turned away from her and stared out at the star-studded sky. "It was one of your stipulations to our marriage."

"And a woman reserves the right to change her mind."

She walked up behind him. With his back to her, she leaned her cheek against his shoulder while slipping her arms around him. Her hand rested over his chest, where she felt the beat of his heart. It was strong and fast.

He cleared his throat, but when he spoke his voice was a bit raspy. "You were very serious that day."

"I'm sorry about that. It was a very emotional day and it crashed in on me."

"I think it's best we stick with the original agreement."

What was that supposed to mean? Her mind jumped to all the wrong conclusions. But then she stopped herself. In the past, jumping to conclusions had done nothing but get her in trouble.

With great trepidation, she asked, "Why is it for the best?"

"You know why."

She pulled back. "No, I don't. But I'd like you to explain it to me."

He shook his head. "Let's not get into this now. It was a nice evening. Let's leave it at that. I'll sleep on the couch. You can have the bed."

"No."

He turned to her. "No, what?"

"No, I'm not going to leave it at that. I want to know what you meant."

"Why do you always have to be so stubborn?"

"I guess I was born that way." She pressed her hands to her hips. "Now quit trying to change the subject."

He raked his fingers through his hair and sighed in defeat. "Because the one night we spent together, I awoke in the morning to find you crying. You regretted our night together. And I don't want a repeat of that experience."

He'd heard her? He'd never said a word about it. If he had, would it have changed things between them? She wasn't sure, but she wanted to clear the air now.

"I wasn't crying because I regretted that you and I had gotten closer. It was quite the opposite. I enjoyed it and that scared me."

"Scared you?"

"Yes. I knew you didn't want a serious relationship. And without us being able to move forward, I knew I would lose you—lose our friendship. I thought I'd once again made a huge mistake. What you saw was me being afraid of losing you."

His eyes searched hers. "Really? That's what you were upset about?"

She nodded. "After all, we've been through thick and thin. I couldn't imagine never speaking to you again."

"You never have to worry about that. I don't know how this whole thing with us is going to work out, but I will always be here for you. That I promise."

"I will be here for you, too. Always and forever."

His head lowered, and he claimed her lips. It seemed so natural, so right. Maybe that was because they were, in fact, newlyweds. Or more likely it was because they'd been made for each other, but one of them had just been too stubborn to see it until now.

But suddenly Luca pulled back. "We shouldn't be doing this."

"We just talked about this. Everything is okay now." She lifted up on her tiptoes to continue the kiss, but Luca leaned back.

"There are still things we need to talk about."

"It can wait. I promise, it'll be all right." She ran her hands up over the front of his shirt to his shoulders, where she slipped off his tux coat. It fell to the floor in a heap. "Tonight isn't for talking."

"It isn't?" His voice was deeper than normal.

"No." She pulled on his bow tie, loosening it. And then she undid the top button of his shirt. "I can think of other, more pressing matters."

"I think I'm getting the idea, but could you be a little clearer about what's on your mind?"

Her fingers undid another button. And then she lifted up on her tiptoes and pressed a trail of kisses along his neck. "Are you getting the idea?"

"Uh-huh." He moved just then and claimed her lips with his own.

This time his kiss wasn't tentative, but rather full of raw desire. As their kiss deepened, hope welled up inside Elena that this was the turning point in their relationship. That, at last, Luca was letting down the walls around his heart and allowing her in. There were still a lot of details to be sorted out, but as long as she knew Luca wanted this marriage for the right reasons, she would meet him halfway.

In the background, the Frank Sinatra love song that had played on their wedding day started up. She would never hear that song again without thinking of this moment. She leaned into Luca like she'd been wanting to do all week. She gave in to the passion that welled up within her, slipping her hands up over his shoulders and wrapping them around the back of his neck. Her fingers combed through his hair.

A kiss had never tasted so good. He tasted of sweet wine and chocolate. His touch was gentle yet needy. Joy filled her knowing that at last they were on the right page.

He pulled back ever so slightly and rested his forehead against hers. "Mrs. DiSalvo, shall we have our wedding night?"

Her heart fluttered. "Oh, yes."

And she sealed it with a kiss. Words were overrated in

this moment. They could communicate lip to lip, hand to hand and body to body.

In the next moment, he swept her up in his arms. With the warm sea breeze caressing them, he carried her over to the four-poster bed draped with a sheer white canopy.

He lowered her onto the fluffy white comforter and stared into her eyes. "It's as if I'm seeing you for the first time."

She smiled up at him. "I hope you like what you see."

"Oh, definitely." But then a worrisome look came over his face.

"What is it?"

"I just don't want to do anything to hurt you."

"You won't." She was trusting him with her heart. "Not unless you don't come closer and kiss me some more."

"That I can do."

He leaned down and pressed his lips to hers.

CHAPTER NINETEEN

THAT HAD BEEN a mistake.

A big one.

Luca slipped out of bed, dressed and went out to stand on the deck overlooking the sea. He shouldn't have let things go so far last night. Sure, he'd wanted Elena more than he'd ever wanted any woman he'd ever known. And yes, they were married, so it was expected.

But what he hadn't done was be totally up front with Elena.

Ever since they'd said their wedding vows, he'd been seeing her in a different light. He'd always thought she was pretty, but now when he looked at her, she took his breath away. And with the pregnancy, she wasn't as thin as she was for the catwalks. He liked those emerging curves a lot—a whole lot.

But he had to tell her that his situation had changed—and not for the better. He was not the man she thought she'd married—

"Hey, what are you doing up so early?" Elena's sleepy voice came from behind him.

He turned around to find her wearing his white dress shirt from last night. The shirt stopped halfway down her thighs. Her long blond hair was tousled. And she'd never looked sweeter.

She reached him and wrapped her arms around his neck before lifting up and pressing a kiss to his lips. Memories of their steamy night together sprang to mind. His body was immediately ready for a repeat.

No. He steeled himself. He was not about to cave again. He had to settle things between them.

Elena pulled away. "Can I get you some coffee?"

"I didn't think you were allowed that now that you're pregnant."

"I'm not. But that doesn't mean I can't get you some. I'll just have some juice or whatever I find in the fridge."

"Oh. Okay. That sounds good." Maybe some caffeine would help straighten his thoughts.

"You know, I've been doing some thinking about our situation," Elena called out from the kitchen. "I'll tell you in a few minutes."

There was a knock at the door.

"I wonder who that can be," Elena said. "I'll get it."

Luca leaned his arms on the railing surrounding the balcony. He stared off in the distance. He couldn't believe that he finally knew what he wanted, but it was just out of his reach.

It was like having an angel on one shoulder and the devil on the other. One prompted him to use his relationship with Elena to gain an audience with the king. It was the only viable way he could get a quick resolution to the lemon grove's troubles.

But the other prompted him to put Elena first. It was a tremendous favor to ask her to get an audience with the king while he was sequestered. The only way to do it would be for her to sneak him in. And that would leave her in a very awkward position with her father.

"These arrived for you." She handed over a newspaper and a big manila envelope.

"Thank you." He glanced at the return address on the envelope. He knew the significance of both items and set them aside.

"Aren't you even going to look at the package? It might be important."

"The envelope contains our wedding photos. I thought you might want them, so I had the photographer rush over the proofs."

"Oh. Okay. And is there any significance to the newspaper?"

He nodded. "We're in it."

"What?" She rushed over, grabbed it and found their photo on the front page. "But how did they get this? The picture is from our wedding at the church."

"I leaked it to the press."

"But why?"

"Because I was tired of their lies. I wanted them to have the truth. Now the world knows we're married."

Her gaze searched his. "You don't care if everyone knows that you married a..." Using air quotes, she said, "'Home wrecker'?"

"You are anything but. In fact, I should make that Steven guy come clean to the world—"

"No! Don't." When he sent her a puzzled look, she added, "It'll just dredge up that mess all over again."

He sighed. "I guess you do have a point. I just hate the thought of him getting away with lying to you."

"He's not. Not exactly. His soon-to-be ex-wife is making sure he's miserable."

"Nothing like a scorned woman."

Elena smiled. "Exactly. I'm sure she can make him squirm in ways you can't even imagine."

"Hmm... I'll have to make sure I don't get on your bad side."

"True." She smiled broadly. "But you don't have anything to worry about after last night. Right now, I feel like anything is possible—"

"Elena, don't go getting too excited."

"Don't worry. I know that we still have steep hurdles to cross. But if you give a little and I give a little, maybe we can meet somewhere in the middle. And our child will win by having both parents in their life."

Guilt assailed Luca. He'd been so caught up in the surprise reception last night and then being alone with Elena that he hadn't been thinking clearly. She'd been so different—so bold. And he was weak when it came to her kisses.

He took a big gulp of coffee. He swallowed, and his stomach churned. Maybe coffee on top of guilt was not a good combination for this morning. He set aside the coffee.

"Elena, come here." He guided her over to the wicker chairs. "There's something I need to tell you."

She looked at him. "I know."

"You do?"

"Yes. Your sister told me last night that you are going to be working with your father in Halencia. So you'll want to spend most of your time there. And that's why I've been thinking—"

"Wait." He waved his hands to gain her attention. "Is that all my sister told you?"

Elena's forehead creased. "What else should she have told me?"

"Nothing. Because she doesn't know this yet."

"Know what? You're worrying me."

He blew out a long breath and leaned forward, placing his elbows on his knees. "There's a problem with the estate. Huge problems."

"What kind of problem?"

"Financial. My father—he ran the estate into debt."

"Oh, no." She reached out and placed her hand on his shoulder. "I'm so sorry to hear this."

Luca's worried gaze met hers. "It isn't like my father to fall behind on his credit payments. He's used the estate, our home, to secure loans—loans that he doesn't have a prayer of paying off."

When Luca chanced a glance at her face, it was pale. She was getting the drift of the severity of the situation.

He didn't want to, but he had to go on. "I've had to use

my savings to stave off the creditors. And now I have nothing to offer you."

"Of course you do. I didn't marry you for your title or your money—"

"But you have a right to expect those things. And I can't give them to you. Well, I still have the title, but at this point it isn't worth much."

"It's okay," she said confidently. "I've got enough money to support both of us and the baby."

"No!" He jumped to his feet and moved to stand by the wall. "I'm not having you do that."

"You mean you're too proud to take money from a woman?"

"No, what I mean is that for a long time I shirked my responsibilities, and I won't do that again. I have to make this right and not take the easy way out. If I did that, if I counted on you to pull me out of this mess, how would our child ever respect me?"

He couldn't just stand there. He knew that Elena must now think less of him for letting things get to this point. If he was a proper son, he would have been there for his father before the business hit this critical juncture.

Luca took off down the steps of the decking bordering the cottage. He didn't have a particular destination in mind. He just needed space to figure out his next step.

"Luca, wait!"

He couldn't face her, not after he'd let her down. He kept going—kept moving down the beach.

"Luca, stop!" Elena cried. "There has to be a way to fix this. We just have to think about it."

Luca begrudgingly stopped and turned to the deck. "I did. And... Oh, never mind."

"No, you were going to say something. I want to know what it is." When she reached him, she placed a finger beneath his chin and lifted until they were eye to eye. "Speak to me."

"The only way to save the estate and the business is to find an immediate influx of cash." Maybe he'd been wrong. Maybe it was his pride and not some do-gooder notion that had him refusing to ask for her help. "I suggested that my father take on a partner with deep pockets, but he outright rejected the idea. He said that this was our legacy and only a DiSalvo would ever own the lemon grove."

"Even if it means losing his business and his home?"

Luca sighed. "Yes. He's a very stubborn man."

"Maybe he sees this as his chance to reconnect with his son."

The same thing had crossed Luca's mind. "I shouldn't have let things get to this point."

When Elena didn't interrupt, he was inclined to expand on his statement. The truth of the matter was that he hadn't opened up to anyone about this part of his life. By not talking about it, sometimes it was easier to pretend that his mother hadn't been stolen away and his family hadn't fractured under the weight of grief.

"It wasn't always this way," he said aloud as a way of convincing himself. "After my mother's death, I needed my father's assurance that everything would be all right—that we would be all right."

Luca drew an unsteady breath as his thoughts rolled back in time. He didn't want to go there and experience the too-familiar pain. Still, he needed Elena to understand how important his endeavor to save the lemon grove was to him. It was his plan to undo some of the damage that had been done to his family.

"My father withdrew from my sister and me. He was cold. He didn't cry. He didn't speak of my mother. I was convinced he didn't love her."

Elena sat down on the beach and patted a spot next to

her. When he joined her, she said, "Maybe he was in shock. I don't know. But anytime I saw your parents together, there was obvious affection."

"I'm starting to think you're right. But back then I was an angry, confused kid. When my sister couldn't get love and assurances from my father, she turned to me, and I failed her."

"You can't blame yourself." Elena reached out and placed her hand over his. "You were so young. It was just too much."

"But I was the oldest. I should have been there for Annabelle. I should have been her rock."

"And because you couldn't be there for your family after your mother's death, you're trying to make up for it now?"

He shrugged and then nodded. Finding warmth and strength in her touch, he laced his fingers with hers. "Do you think it's too late?"

"No. I think saving your family's business is heroic."

"But I haven't accomplished it yet. The only option I can think of is to gain one of Mirraccino's contracts. They are lucrative and far-reaching with their export business. I talked with Demetrius, but he said that they are experiencing a full audit after what the king's lord-in-waiting did to my mother. There's fear that he was embezzling from the crown. Demetrius said he couldn't do anything for me now, but that we could revisit it in the future. The problem is that will take too long. The creditors will call in their loans before then. The only way to get around Demetrius's decision is to go directly to the king, but I can't get to him."

"And you need my help to get access to him."

Luca nodded.

Now it was up to Elena. And he had no idea how she would feel about pulling strings with her father in order to help him. He hated to put her in this position, but at that moment, he just couldn't think of any other plan.

CHAPTER TWENTY

Talk about stressful.

Luca had been in a lot of tense business meetings, but this one was the worst.

He sat on a wing-back chair in the king's suite of rooms. He hadn't been in here since he was a little kid, and to be honest, it was still a bit intimidating as an adult. The room was regally decorated, mostly in maroon, with cream-colored walls. The furniture was all antique and he couldn't even begin to guess their ages, but every item was well maintained.

The king was up and dressed, but he looked to be a shell of the man that Luca once knew. Luca couldn't decide if it was age or stress or a little of both.

Luca had given his uncle an overview of the challenges facing the DiSalvo family. He had brought some projections with him, but he knew not to present them unless invited. As of yet, no invitation had been extended. The king had merely listened and nodded at the appropriate moments. And now that Luca had said everything that he'd come here to say, silence filled the room.

After a few moments, the king said, "Luca, I am sorry I haven't been around, especially as I hear that you and Elena have married. I want to offer you my best wishes."

"Thank you, sir. We appreciate it."

"I hadn't realized that you two were seeing each other. But then again, I haven't exactly been accessible recently. But I thought that Elena's father would have mentioned it."

Luca swallowed hard. "Actually, it was a bit of a whirlwind relationship, and we sort of kept it to ourselves."

"I can understand. Once upon a time I was a young man. Things can happen quickly." The king stared off into the distance as though he was caught up in memories. "I've watched Elena grow up, and there's something very special about her. She'll make you a good wife. You take care of that girl."

"I will, sir." This was his chance to get the conversation back on track. *Please let him agree.* "That's why I'm trying to secure a deal for the lemon grove."

"About that, I am sorry. But my son is right. We cannot grant new contracts right now. The kingdom's records and finances are all under review. Everything is on hold at the moment."

"I understand." He might understand, but that didn't make his situation any better.

"Once every file and account has been audited to make sure that criminal didn't embezzle or sell any national secrets, our security will return to normal and new business will commence. If you could just wait, we will give your proposal due consideration."

Luca couldn't just walk away. Even though the king couldn't help him now, he wanted to do or say something to help his uncle, or to just let him know that he wasn't alone. "Sir, you know that what happened with my mother wasn't your fault. And no one blames you."

The king's tired eyes widened. "How can people not blame me? That murderer worked for me. He was right here in this palace." A sorrowful expression filled his face. "I am so sorry this happened to your mother. I can't express enough my sorrow and regret that this happened."

How exactly did he respond to that? Luca never blamed him. "I appreciate your words, but you don't need to apologize."

"I should have known something was wrong." His fist pounded on the arm of his chair. "What kind of ruler am I if I can miss something so important?"

"You are human like the rest of us. Please believe me that

no one in my family—or in the palace or, for that matter, the nation—blames you. But people do miss you."

"Thank you. I will take that under consideration."

After thanking the king again for seeing him, Luca made his exit. He was in no better position than when he'd arrived. But he was in no worse shape, either.

And yet, he could feel everything he'd strived for slipping away. His childhood home, his legacy—it all now hung in a very precarious position. And should he fail to save it, he imagined that he would lose contact with his father and sister once more. This was why he kept people at a distance. Letting them in just set him up for more pain.

Most important, he would lose all of his savings on this venture and have no way to support Elena and the baby. He raked his fingers through his hair. If this was the best he could do, then perhaps he didn't deserve this family.

As he made his way out of the palace, he knew he would find a way to make this all work. He had to. Everyone was counting on him.

The deed was done.

Elena couldn't believe she'd begged her father to let Luca speak with the king. She knew her father didn't want to do it, but she'd pleaded with him and told him that her entire future was on the line. He'd asked if it was really that important, and she'd promised that it was. She knew that if Luca didn't save his legacy, their marriage didn't stand a chance of surviving—if it ever had.

She sure hoped Luca knew what he was doing. He seemed so certain the king would help that she wondered what would happen if the king's hands were tied just as his son's were. Elena didn't know a lot about how the government worked, but something told her the king would not override the crown prince's decision, not when the king was positioning his son to take over the kingdom—at least, that was what her father had led her to believe.

After stopping by to check on her mother, Elena retrieved her sketch pad and colored pencils. If nothing else, she could get some work done. Now that her modeling contract with Lauren Renard had been dissolved, Elena needed to focus on her new career path—designing her own fashions.

When she arrived back at the cottage, it was empty. Luca still hadn't returned. She'd taken that as a good sign—the king was hearing him out. And though Luca didn't go on and on about his family's business being in danger and what that would mean to his father, she knew it had Luca tied up in knots. If it was possible to get the lemon grove on level financial ground, would Luca be more open about his feelings toward the baby? And her?

But Elena foresaw a problem with his plan. Luca was trying to take on this enormous problem all by himself. Granted, she wasn't that familiar with the business world, but to her it seemed like the more people you had brainstorming ways to solve a problem, the quicker and easier the solution would be derived.

She grabbed her phone and selected Annabelle's number. Elena hesitated before she pressed Send. Sure, Annabelle had invited her to her engagement festivities, but how would she feel about Elena inserting herself into family business? Would she be willing to talk to Elena about something so intrinsic to her family?

There was only one way to find out. Elena pressed the button. The phone rang once, twice...

"Hey, Elena, I was just thinking about you." Annabelle's cheerful voice came over the line.

"You were?"

"Uh-huh. I was wondering how the impromptu honeymoon is going."

Elena paused, not sure what to say.

"Elena, is something wrong?"

This was her opening. She just had to take it. "That's the thing—the honeymoon, it's not going so well."

"I'm so sorry. Is there anything I can do?"

"Actually, there is. I need to talk to you about Luca—"

"Elena, who are you talking to?" Luca's voice boomed across the room.

Elena jumped. She hadn't even heard him enter the cottage. She turned to find a dark look on his face. She wondered just how much he'd overheard.

She held up a finger to get him to wait and then she spoke into the phone. "I've got to go."

"I'm here whenever you need to talk."

"Thanks. I appreciate that." Elena disconnected the call. She turned to Luca. "I didn't hear you come in."

"Obviously." His tone rumbled with agitation. "What exactly were you planning to say before I interrupted?"

Elena felt bad that he'd misinterpreted what he'd overheard. "It was nothing bad."

He crossed his arms and waited.

"I was talking with your sister and I was going to see if she had some ideas of what to do about the lemon grove."

"Why would she have any ideas?" His brows drew together in a formidable line. "This isn't her problem."

"The last time I checked, she was part of your family, and the lemon grove does belong to your family."

"But this is my problem, not hers...and not yours."

His last words stabbed at her heart. Even though they'd gotten married, made mad, passionate love and she was carrying his child, Luca still refused to let her in. What was his problem? When was he going to learn that people weren't out to hurt him?

In this moment, she felt as though she was fighting for the future of her marriage. "This *is* my problem. I'm your

wife, remember. And it's your sister and your father's problem. What is wrong with you? Why can't you let people in?"

"I don't need to let people in. I do fine on my own."

She lifted her chin. "If you're so fine, why do you look
so miserable?"

"Because I came home to find my wife doesn't believe
that I can take care of our family."

"And so you're going to stand on your pride instead of
reaching out for help."

"I don't need help. Just leave me alone."

Really? This was how he was going to play it? He'd been
pushing her away for too long now. And she wasn't going
to put up with it anymore.

"Luca, I love you. I want to help you. What is so wrong
with that?"

He shook his head, and his gaze didn't meet hers. "I
didn't ask for anyone to take pity on me."

"It's not pity. It's what people do when they love each
other." And then she realized that the night they'd spent
together might have meant something totally different to
him than it had to her. "Luca, do you love me?"

He didn't say anything. And then he walked toward the
balcony. If he thought he was getting away and avoiding
this, he was wrong. She followed him.

"Luca." When he didn't even acknowledge that he'd
heard her, she tried again. "Luca, answer me."

He turned to her. "I can't tell you what you want to hear.
I can't be the man you want me to be."

Tears pricked the backs of her eyes, but she refused to
give in to her pregnancy hormones. She blinked back the
moisture. She refused to let Luca see how much his words
hurt her.

"You might not love me, but you can't say the same
about your family."

"I don't need them, either. Why do you think I can't be happy alone?"

"Because I believe that everyone needs somebody. I have to believe that, otherwise…" She stopped as her emotions threatened to overtake her.

"Otherwise what?" His intent gaze studied her as though trying to ferret out the truth.

She swallowed hard. "Otherwise you won't be able to love our child."

He didn't say a word. Not one syllable. Instead he turned to stare out at the sea.

That's it! She had tried to be understanding, but she'd had enough of his stubborn attitude. If he couldn't meet her halfway, she was done.

"You know, you don't have to face the world alone." She held back from saying that she would stand by his side through anything. "Your family would rally around you if you'd let them in. That's what families do."

He turned to her. His eyes were dark, and his stance was rigid. "And what makes you think I need their help?"

"A better question is how are you supposed to be a loving parent to our baby if you never let anyone in?"

"Stop saying that." He stared at her as though shocked that she would say these things to him. "I do let people in."

"No, you don't." She didn't know why she bothered. He'd counted on himself for so long now that he didn't know any other way to be. "I give up. I love you, but obviously that's never going to penetrate the wall around your heart."

He looked at her, but he didn't say anything. This was where he should profess his love for her, too. And yet there was nothing but a stony silence.

Though it was breaking her heart, she just couldn't imprison him or herself in a one-sided marriage. She knew he would stay out of obligation, and if she didn't walk out that door right now, he would be miserable for the rest of his life. And she loved him too much to do that to him.

"I can't do this anymore." She turned for the door.

"Where are you going?"

"At last, you speak. If you must know, I'm going to my parents' for dinner. They invited us both, but I can't imagine that you would want to go. I'll give them your regrets." She continued to the door. And then she paused and turned. "I guess this is goodbye."

"Goodbye?"

"Yes. Tomorrow I'm returning to Paris. I'll email you with any important information about the baby. Goodbye, Luca."

She turned and headed out the door while she could still maintain a dignified expression. Because that had been the hardest thing she'd ever done in her life. Her heart felt as though it had been ripped from her chest.

CHAPTER TWENTY-ONE

WHAT HAD JUST HAPPENED?

Luca stared at the closed door as he gathered his thoughts. In the heat of the moment, he decided Elena leaving was for the best.

He paced back and forth in the cottage, feeling like a caged animal. Why did everyone in his life keep telling him that he was doing things the wrong way? All he was trying to do was stand on his own two legs. Was that such a bad thing?

Of course not.

He contemplated walking out the door and not stopping. He needed away from the palace and Mirraccino—away from Elena. But for the first time ever, he couldn't imagine being on his own again. Every time he thought of the future, he saw Elena in it.

The voices of Elena, his father, the king and others echoed in his head. He had to get out of there. He headed for the beach. The sounds of the water, the birds and the breeze were calming. Now he had to unravel this tangled mess, because so much was at stake.

Never before had he had this many people foisting their opinions and advice upon him. All of them wanted him to do this or that, but none asked what he wanted to do.

The last time—the only time—he'd done what he was told, it had been with his mother. He didn't let himself think of her very often, but her memory filled his mind now. He reached for the chain that hung around his neck, a constant reminder of her—a source of comfort in times of trouble. He removed the chain from his neck and clutched the St. Christopher medal in his palm.

When he was a child, his mother was the only one to

guide him—to tell him what needed to be done. His sister had been too little, his father too busy and Elena too awestruck by the fact that he was a part of the royal family.

In the years since his mother's murder, he'd been doing his best to navigate life on his own. Was it possible that in his efforts to avoid another loss that he'd built these walls around himself that Elena mentioned?

He supposed it was true. He'd never really stopped to think about it. But it was the only way he knew how to be. He didn't even know how to change.

But if he didn't do something, he was going to lose the woman he loved. It was the first time he'd allowed himself to admit his intense feelings for Elena to himself. And instead of it being scary, it was freeing. It was like stepping out of the shadows and into the sunlight.

He knew she still had the ability to hurt him, but by denying his feelings, he was hurting himself more. But was it too late? Would she give him a second chance?

He had to prove to her that he'd changed—that he was willing to let people into his life. And he knew how to do it. He would start with his father and sister.

He had an idea of how to save the lemon grove, but he couldn't do it by himself. Finally, he was hearing what Elena had been telling him. He wasn't in this battle alone. There were people around who wanted to help, if he'd let them.

First, he would speak to his father, Annabelle and the newest member of the family, Grayson. When Luca went to Elena, he was going to show her that family meant everything to him.

Elena and the baby were his everything.

CHAPTER TWENTY-TWO

ELENA HAD ARRIVED home early for dinner.

She had nowhere else to go and nothing she wanted to do. And since she was leaving in the morning, she thought she would spend the extra time with her mother.

"Dear, you really don't have to help with dinner. I can manage," her mother insisted as she tried to prepare food while balancing on her crutches.

"Mother, why don't you sit at the table and I'll bring you whatever you need?"

"Well, that probably would be easier. Thanks." She moved to the table. "But something tells me you have more on your mind than worrying about me. For a newlywed, you've been spending a lot of time at home. What's going on?"

Elena didn't know how to respond. She just wasn't willing to admit to anyone that her brief marriage was a bust. Every time she thought of vocalizing the words, the backs of her eyes started to sting. She couldn't avoid the subject forever, but for just this moment, she wanted to pretend that her heart wasn't breaking in two.

Elena started slicing cheese. "Can I ask you something?"

"Sure. Does it have to do with sex?"

The knife slipped, barely missing Elena's finger. "Mother!"

"Okay. I was just kidding." Her mother sat at the table cutting orange wedges for the fruit and cheese tray.

Elena kept her gaze on the task at hand, not wanting her mother to read too much in her gaze. "When you first got married, did you— Well, was Father a little distant?"

"Your father? No. He's always been romantic and passionate—"

"Mother, I thought we said we weren't going there."

Her mother laughed. "Passionate about his feelings, daughter. I've always known where I stood with him."

Which just reinforced her decision to end things with Luca. She never knew where she stood with him, and she couldn't live like that.

"I take it you and Luca are having some problems adjusting."

"Something like that." Maybe if she opened up a little more, her mother would be able to give her some helpful advice. After all, her mother knew how to maintain a successful marriage. "It's just that he won't open up and let me in. And now that I'm—"

She stopped. How could she just go and almost blurt out that she was pregnant? Now wasn't the time for that news.

"You really are pregnant, aren't you?" The glee was obvious in her mother's voice. She got to her feet in record time and rushed over to put an arm around Elena. "I'm so happy for you."

When they pulled apart, Elena said, "No one knows."

"Haven't you told your husband?"

"He knows." Since she'd already said more than she intended, she might as well finish confessing. "It's the only reason he married me."

"What?" Her mother sounded shocked. "Surely you don't believe that."

"How can I not believe it? I asked him once if he loved me, and he said no."

"But that can't be right. I've watched you two over the years. It's as plain to me as the nose on my face that you two belong together. I just wondered how long it would take you to figure it out."

Elena sniffled. "I figured it out, but he didn't. And I can't live with someone who doesn't love me back. It's not right for me, and it's not right for our baby."

"Oh, Elena, think hard before you do anything drastic. Sometimes we only get one chance at love."

The sound of footsteps had them both turning. There in the entrance to the kitchen stood Luca. He looked awful. His face was pale and drawn. Elena's first instinct was to go to him, but she held herself back. If this was going to work, he had to make the first move.

"I knocked," he said, "but I don't think anyone heard, so I let myself in. I hope that's all right."

"Of course it is," her mother said, as though there wasn't a thing wrong. "You're family now. You are welcome here anytime."

"Thank you." His gaze met Elena's. "That means a lot."

Her mother smiled. "I hope you brought your appetite. Elena and I have been cooking up a storm. We can eat as soon as my husband arrives."

Elena stood by quietly, wondering what his real reason was for being there. Part of her was frustrated and she didn't want to have the same argument with him again. But another part of her wondered if maybe her words had finally gotten through to him.

"Actually," Luca said, "I was wondering if I could borrow your daughter for a little bit."

"Certainly. She's all done here."

When Elena didn't make any movement to go to him, Luca said, "Elena, there are things I need to say to you. It's important."

He deserved to wait a minute. She wanted him to know that she wasn't going to jump every time he called. Most of all, he had to know that he'd truly hurt her.

"Please," he pleaded.

That was what she needed. She turned to her mother. "Are you sure you've got everything?"

"Positive. Thank you for your help. I appreciate it and our chat. Now go." She shooed them from the kitchen. As they were going out the door, her mother hollered, "And if you don't make it back this evening, we'll have leftovers tomorrow."

Oh, her mother, ever the optimistic one.

Elena wasn't as hopeful. Maybe she was building up her own walls now. But she just couldn't get her hopes up and let her heart get broken all over again.

CHAPTER TWENTY-THREE

LUCA HAD NEVER been more nervous in his life.

Neither said a word as they walked. He didn't have a destination in mind. He just needed time alone with Elena. And now that he was with her, the words inside him twisted up in a knot and clogged his throat.

Their meandering led them to the cliff overlooking the sea. The sun hovered on the horizon, sending magnificent shades of pink and purple streaking through the sky. But nothing could hold a candle to his wife's beauty.

And if he didn't say the right things now, he knew he was going to lose her for good. His chance at having a family would be gone. And he didn't know how he would live with the knowledge that he'd ruined it all.

He swallowed hard. "Elena, please don't do this. Don't leave."

She maintained a considerable distance between them. Her gaze was cool and distant. "I want you to know that I really appreciate all you've done for me. Not many men would have stepped up and proposed marriage to protect their unborn baby from a scandal."

"I did what I needed to do. And I'd do it again."

"But that's the thing—you don't need to do anything else. The crisis has been averted. We can now go back to our lives."

"Elena, please don't do this."

"I can't continue to live a lie. If we can't fully and honestly communicate with each other, we can't have a healthy marriage."

"Listen, I'm sorry about not telling you about my family's financial crisis as soon as I learned about it. But thanks to you, we have a plan in place to get us through this rough patch. I just came from talking to my father, Annabelle and Grayson. We are going to contract with Fo Shizzle Cafés for as much produce as they can take. And we spoke with Demetrius, who was able to give us a date for when the royal family will start taking on new contracts again. He said ours would be the first they considered."

Elena shook her head. "You're still not hearing me. I'm not talking about business."

"But I reached out to my family for help. Isn't that what you wanted?"

"Partly. But you still won't let anyone know how you feel."

He raked his fingers through his hair. "And how do you want me to resolve that?"

"I don't know. I'm not sure it can be resolved. That's why I'm going back to Paris in the morning."

"You mean alone?"

"Yes. It's best for everyone."

Again, there was a coolness to her words. Her voice was almost monotone, and he noticed how her gaze didn't quite meet his. He felt like she was blocking him out—like he was suddenly a stranger to her. And he didn't like it. Not one little bit.

He wanted his Elena back—the person who made him laugh, who was full of emotion and tenderness. This aloofness wasn't like her.

And then it dawned on him that this was how it must have been for Elena to deal with him all this time. It was as if he suddenly truly understood what his efforts to protect himself had done to those around him.

"Elena, I am sorry for blocking you out. I was afraid. Afraid of losing you from my life, whether it be an unexpected death or indifference or something else. I'm not afraid to love you anymore."

She stood there much like a statue. She didn't say anything. In fact, she didn't react at all. Hadn't she heard him? "Elena, I love you."

CHAPTER TWENTY-FOUR

SHE'D HEARD HIM.

She'd tried not to, but his words penetrated her heart.

She didn't react right away, because she was still processing this information. It was a lot to take in. And they had to get this right.

Elena lifted her chin. "Are you saying all this because you now feel that you have something to offer?"

"What?"

"The deal with the lemon grove. Are you willing to take a risk on us because you want your child to grow up on the DiSalvo estate?"

"No. No. No. Didn't you hear me? I love you. I know it took a long time for me to get it all straight, but I'm here now, asking you to forgive me. I've made a lot of mistakes, but I never meant to hurt you."

Her heart fluttered. These were the words she'd been longing to hear for so very long. A tear splashed onto her cheek. She swiped it away.

Luca got down on one knee and took her hand in his. "I did this once and I meant it, but I didn't get it exactly right, so I'd like a do-over. Is that all right?"

She nodded as a smile pulled at her lips. At last, the wall around his heart had crumbled. Her heart pounded with love and joy.

"Elena, I love you. If I am honest with myself, I've always loved you. When something good happens, you're the first person I think of to tell. If something bad happens, you're the one I want to share my troubles. Yours is the last face I want to see at night and the first in the morning. I want to spend the rest of my days showing you just how much I love you. Will you spend the rest of your life with me?"

"Yes. Yes. Yes." She drew him up to his feet. "I love you with all my heart." And then she took his hand and pressed it to her abdomen. "We both do."

Luca stared deep into her eyes. "I'm the luckiest man in the world."

"And I am the luckiest woman. I get to spend the rest of my life with my best friend."

She lifted up on her tiptoes and pressed her lips to his.

EPILOGUE

Eleven months later

ELENA STOOD IN the gardens of the royal palace. Annabelle and Grayson had just been married. Elena and Luca had stood up for them. And the king had attended, now that he was back to being himself.

It was so nice to be back in Mirraccino. She said that every time she and Luca visited, which was often. As much as she loved Halencia, it would never have that special something that Mirraccino did. Maybe it was because this was her childhood home…or maybe it was because it was here that she'd met the man of her dreams, who at that point had been a little boy who didn't mind getting his formal clothes dirty playing with a girl. Elena smiled at the memories. They seemed so long ago now.

While Luca talked with one of his many cousins, Elena excused herself. European football was something that still didn't interest her—no matter how much Luca tried to sway her. Although she had enjoyed playing football with Luca as a kid, it didn't hold her attention in the same way. Now the only thing she recognized about the game was which jersey matched which team. What could she say? Fashion was in her blood. Only in a different way now.

She moved around the vast gardens. The walkways were lit up with torches that gave a soft glow to the fragrant foliage. Their garden in Halencia was just as beautiful, but not nearly as vast. It was where Elena spent a lot of time now that their son, Marco, had been born. Instead of modeling glamorous fashions, she was now doing something she loved—designing. Her debut fashion show was planned for this fall. She couldn't wait.

When fingers wrapped around her shoulders, she jumped.

"Hey, relax. It's just me," Luca murmured very close to her ear. Then he leaned over and pressed his lips to the nape of her neck. "What had you so deep in thought?"

"I was just thinking about the path we took to get here. It's hard to believe that we once played hide-and-seek in these gardens and now your sister is having her wedding reception here."

"I was beginning to wonder if she was ever going to get married—"

"Luca, really. Just because you rushed me down the aisle doesn't mean everyone wants to elope."

"Are you saying you regret our rush to the altar?"

"Of course not." She lifted up on her tiptoes and pressed her lips to his. "I love you, Luca. With all my heart."

"I love you, too." He kissed her again. "Are you sure you don't want a wedding do-over?"

"I'm positive. But I must admit that if I was going to have a wedding, I'd want it to be like this one, even if it took your sister a year to plan."

Luca glanced around. "I guess it isn't too bad."

Elena lightly punched him on the shoulder. "It's gorgeous. I'm so happy for your sister."

"I'm thinking I might have to hire her."

"For what?"

"I want to throw a party."

Elena frowned at her husband. "I told you I don't want to get married again. We got it right the first time, even if it took us a little bit to figure it out."

"Who said anything about getting married again?" He arched a dark brow. "I'm thinking that we have our first anniversary coming up and it deserves a party."

"You really want to go to all that trouble?"

Luca drew her close in his arms. "Mrs. DiSalvo, haven't

you figured out that I would go to the moon and back for you?"

She tilted her chin up. "I wouldn't let you get that far away."

Between his sweet words and the way he stared deeply into her eyes, her heart tap-danced in her chest and her knees became rubbery. She loved the way he could still make her feel as giddy as she had when this whole love affair began.

"Why's that?" he asked.

"Because I couldn't bear to be separated from you for that long."

"Don't worry. I'll always be right here." He pressed his hand to her heart.

She lifted up on her tiptoes and pressed her lips to his. Her heart swelled with love. She didn't know it was possible to love someone this much.

A lifetime together would never be enough.

* * * * *

If you loved this novel, you won't want to miss
THE MILLIONAIRE'S ROYAL RESCUE,
the first book in Jennifer Faye's
MIRRACCINO MARRIAGES *duet.*
Available now!

If you want another marriage of convenience
romance, make sure to watch out for
BOUND TO THE GREEK BILLIONAIRE by Rebecca
Winters, the second book in her
THE BILLIONAIRE'S CLUB *trilogy.*